ALSO BY HUGH PENTECOST

Pierre Chambrun Mystery Novels:
WALKING DEAD MAN
BIRTHDAY, DEATHDAY
THE DEADLY JOKE
GIRL WATCHER'S FUNERAL
THE GILDED NIGHTMARE
THE GOLDEN TRAP
THE EVIL MEN DO
THE SHAPE OF FEAR
THE CANNIBAL WHO OVERATE

Julian Quist Mystery Novels:
THE CHAMPAGNE KILLER
DON'T DROP DEAD TOMORROW

John Jericho Mystery Novels:
A PLAGUE OF VIOLENCE
THE GIRL WITH SIX FINGERS
DEAD WOMAN OF THE YEAR
THE CREEPING HOURS
HIDE HER FROM EVERY EYE
SNIPER

The Beautiful Dead

The Beautiful Dead

A Red Badge Novel of Suspense

HUGH PENTECOST

DODD, MEAD & COMPANY · NEW YORK

ISBN: 0-396-06865-0
Library of Congress Catalog Card Number: 73-11551
Printed in the United States of America
by Vail-Ballou Press, Inc., Binghamton, N. Y.

Part One

chapter 1

It was a hot August night. To be quite exact, it was a hot August morning—two-thirty in the morning. There was a moon, almost full, almost red as it hung on the rim of the sky. It was reflected in the hourglass-shaped swimming pool where two heads bobbed in the pale light which penetrated the darkness with a kind of gentle insistence. The air was heavy with the scent of flowers, particularly from the wisteria which grew over the bathhouses at the far end of the pool. A hundred yards away, across an expanse of beautifully cared-for lawn, was a great stone house, ivy covering its walls. A few lights showed at its windows, but quite obviously most of the household had gone to bed.

The swimmers in the pool weren't active. One was a man, one was a woman. They were both as naked as babes. They floated side by side. The man turned his golden-blond head toward the dark-haired girl and reached out to touch her tenderly. They were at the shallow end of the pool, and

3

suddenly they were standing very close together, their arms around each other. It was a moment of love, not passion. The man took his lips away from the girl's mouth and walked toward the edge of the pool. The girl reached out a hand in a gesture that suggested his going away was regretted, now and always when he went away.

The man pulled himself up out of the pool and walked along the edge toward a table and chairs a few yards away. He picked up a terry-cloth robe on one of the chairs and fished in the wide pockets. He produced a slim cigar case and a gold lighter. He took a long, thin cigar from the case and put it in his mouth. He spun the lighter into flame. But he didn't light the cigar.

The flame had called his attention to something. He stood like a statue, looking at a hand, palm up, that protruded from behind a clump of lilac bushes a few yards away. There were no sounds that weren't a part of the night —the chattering of crickets, the almost human cry of some night bird at a distance, the steady noise of water spilling out of the pool into an overflow channel. The hand didn't move.

The man reached down and picked up the robe. He put it on. He slipped his feet into a pair of sandals and walked toward the lilac bushes. He moved around to the far side and looked down.

"Jesus!" he whispered.

He bent down and, once again, flicked on the lighter. He didn't move or say anything more. The flame died out. He stood up and went back to the table and chairs. He picked up a second robe and pair of sandals. He went back to the edge of the pool where the dark-haired girl floated in the water.

"Change your mind about coming back, Julian?" the girl asked.

"Out you come, darling," the man said.

She came without question. She stood beside him, glistening wet in the moonlight. He held the robe for her and put down her sandals so she could step into them. Then his hands closed on her upper arms, not gently.

"Lydia, Caroline is over there behind those lilac bushes."

The girl laughed. "Darling, I'm sure she's seen people in the nude before."

"She's dead, Lydia." His voice was harsh.

"Oh, my God, Julian!"

"Very violently dead. Somebody chose to cut her to pieces."

"Julian!"

"I want you to go up to the house. Go around the other side of the pool. I don't want you to have to see her."

"But I—"

"Go, doll. This is a police matter. I want you to call them. Tell them it's a homicide. I'll stay here—to make sure no one comes back."

"But how, Julian? We didn't hear a sound."

"It happened before we got out here."

"Don't I call Mark?"

"Let the police wake him," the man said. "Make the call and then go up to our room and dress. We won't be sleeping tonight." He bent down and kissed her forehead. "Go!"

He watched her move round the pool and up across the lawn. Then he lit the long thin cigar. He stood very still, staring toward the bushes, a cloud of pale blue smoke circling his blond head.

* * *

It had all started on such a gay level. The offices of Julian Quist Associates, located in a glass finger pointing to the sky high above Grand Central Station in New York City, were as "mod" as Quist himself and the group of people who surrounded him. The colors were pale pastels. The furniture, promising discomfort, turned out to be delightfully comfortable and functional. Paintings on the walls represented the most current artists, all very much "with it." The reception room was presided over by the striking Miss Gloria Chard, wearing her simple little Rudi Gernreich creations, looking as if she had been put together by some genius in the art of female allure.

On the day it began, Lydia was in Quist's private office along with Constance Parmalee, Quist's secretary, and Marilyn Martin, the famous dress designer. Quist, wearing a pale blue linen suit with a yellow turtle-neck knit shirt, leaned back in his desk chair, smoking one of his long, thin cigars, his eyes half closed. He was only half listening to the three women. Lydia, looking more like a high-fashion model than a brilliant researcher and writer for the firm, was his—dark, sultry, provocative. On the second floor of his duplex apartment there was a room that belonged to Lydia. There was a clothes closet, a dressing table with theatrical make-up lights, a bureau, a chaise longue. But no bed. The only bed in the apartment was a king-sized model in Quist's room. Lydia had her own apartment a couple of blocks away, but she was rarely there.

Miss Parmalee, the secretary, was a slim girl with red hair and a good figure and legs that justified the wearing of a mini-skirt. She looked at the world through faintly tinted granny glasses.

Marilyn Martin was something else again; a woman of

6

fifty-five who admits to being ten years younger. She was super-smart, marvelously turned out, her hair changing color with her collection of stylish wigs. Her voice was roughened by too many cigarettes and too many martinis, her tongue sharp, her wit acidulous.

"I have seen all the *Last Tangos*," Marilyn was saying, "I know all the words, all the positions, all the techniques. Now I have become an incurable romantic. I like men to send me flowers; I like them to hold a door open for me, or pull back my chair. I like to be courted with elegance."

Woman talk. It could be irritating, Quist thought, like a steam drill, or it could be a kind of pleasant meaningless chatter that you enjoyed because you were fond of the people making the noise. I am, he thought, a male chauvinist pig.

"I am sick of youth!" Marilyn said. "For me glamor is the result of a life experience. Nothing that modern youth does with all its freedoms, sexual and otherwise, was overlooked by my generation. There's nothing attractive about today's life style. I'm going to bring back the mature glamor girl—the Carole Lombard, Joan Crawford, Irene Dunne, Norma Shearer image."

"You're not that old," Quist said.

"But I stay up for the late movies," Marilyn said. "Clothes are only a fraction of what makes a female fashionable. It is also her figure, her hairdo, her morality, and her philosophy of life."

"You are quoting another Marilyn," Lydia said. "Marylin spelled with a "y," Marylin Bender who writes about The Beautiful People for the *New York Times*."

"I steal from anyone if it suits me," Marilyn said. "In the sixties fashion stopped being clothes and became a value, a

7

tool, a way of life, a kind of symbolism. Clothes are not designed to keep people warm or dry, but to make them sexually attractive."

"You quote," Lydia said.

"Bitch," Marilyn said cheerfully.

"You didn't come here to deliver a lecture, love," Quist said.

"I came here to hire you to do a job," Marilyn said. "I am going to bring out a new line of glamor clothes for the mature doll. Now, to whip up a desire for something people don't really need, particularly in mass quantities, glamorous idols are necessary. There have to be people in high places that thousands of women would like to imitate. Like Jacqueline Kennedy in the sixties. I want you to create for me a goddess of fashion."

"Specifications?" Quist asked.

"Physical beauty, wealth and social position, to be seen everywhere that's important—the right parties, the right charity functions, the places the girl-in-the-street thinks of as glamorous—Acapulco, Las Vegas, opening nights on Broadway. She must be special, but not snooty; aloof and yet approachable."

"I suggest Lydia," Quist said, looking at the luscious dark girl.

"Physical beauty, yes," Marilyn said. "Style, yes. But unfortunately she isn't rich and she's living in sin with you."

Quist's blue eyes stayed on the dark girl. "If what we have together is sinful," he said, "I hereby cancel my application for a harp and halo."

"I love you both," Marilyn said. "Be serious, please."

Quist flicked the ash from his cigar into a brass tray on his desk. "Jacqueline Kennedy had some special assets beyond your specifications," he said. "She was married to the most important man in the world at that time. She, as first lady, was covered by every photographer in the United States and abroad. Every move she made, every dress she wore, was photographed. She didn't have to ask for coverage. She got it whether she liked it or not."

"Find me the right woman and you can make her just as watched, just as fascinating."

"Rich, beautiful, thirtyish, socially prominent," Miss Parmalee said, taking notes.

"Not living in sin," Quist said, looking at Lydia. "Are you thinking of the same person I am, love?"

"Caroline Stillwell," Lydia said.

"Mark Stillwell's wife?" Marilyn asked, her eyes hawk-bright.

"A moderately successful movie star who retired for love," Quist said. "She married a prince in the world of finance. She has a house in New York, a house in Westchester, a house in Palm Beach, an apartment in London. She is beautiful, stylish, about thirty-five. She's almost another Grace Kelly, if you care."

"Prince of finance!" Marilyn snorted. "Today's millionaires aren't the great barons and pirates who made this country work. They make their money in intricate financial manipulations. They're no more than imaginative bookkeepers."

"Not every man can get to bc President of the United States or the Prince of Monaco," Lydia said. "Anyway, they pay the bills."

"This isn't quite the same as those two dolls," Marilyn said. "They made designers and couturiers famous by wearing their clothes. The ones whose clothes they wore were just fabulously lucky. This is different. You've got to persuade her to wear my clothes, and be seen where you tell her to be seen, do what you tell her to do. It's not going to be luck. She's got to agree to play along with us. Why did you think of Caroline Stillwell, you two?"

"Because we know her," Quist said. "She was once a client—when she was in films. I can put it right on the table for her, without having to play games. Either she will or she won't."

"But why should she?" Marilyn asked.

"Because your clothes will be marvelous," Quist said. "Because no woman can resist having stylish new outfits for every occasion on every day. Because no woman could feel anything but pleasure in becoming a public glamor symbol. Because she might find it fun. And because she might do a favor for a friend. How much cash are you willing to put on the line?"

Marilyn's eyebrows rose. "She already has a zillion dollars!"

"You might be surprised at how much a rich man's wife would like to have a little pocket money of her own," Quist said. "From your point of view it would make the contract more binding."

"I'd leave that to you," Marilyn said. "What's her husband like—Mark Stillwell?"

"He's a preoccupied dreamboat," Lydia said. "Handsome, athletic-looking, but preoccupied."

"If he's too preoccupied to pay attention to you, dear, he's a queer," Marilyn said.

Lydia looked at Quist. "Maybe he's afraid of Julian," she said.

Marilyn pointed a jeweled finger at her. "If your life of

10

sin turns other men off, you'll regret it."

"I'd be desolate if no one made passes at me," Lydia said. "Julian might think I wasn't worth keeping. But Mark Stillwell is climbing a golden ladder up into the sky. Until he reaches the top, nothing else matters."

"The trouble is he doesn't realize there is no end to the climb," Quist said.

"Doesn't he care for his wife? I don't want marital scandals in the picture," Marilyn said.

"He cares for her," Quist said, frowning. "She's an important status symbol to him. She makes him a very male figure. More important, she's in love with him and ready to wait for him to reach the top. It's worth talking to her, Marilyn. She might find it was something amusing to do while she waits. The worst that can happen is that she says 'no,' and then we look for someone else."

Marilyn stood up and turned toward the door. "It's your ball game, Julian. Please, God, let your bill be reasonable."

The next day Quist took two beautiful women to lunch. They made quite a stir as they walked into Willard's Back Yard, Quist's favorite summer lunching spot. There was, actually, a tree-shaded back yard. Heads turned as Willard himself led them through the main room to a table in the so-called garden area. Lydia, dark, sultry, exotic, and Caroline Stillwell, a natural redhead with high cheekbones, a wide generous mouth, and gray-green eyes, expertly shadowed, flanked Quist, tall, his gold-blond hair worn longish but expertly styled, his dark blue club blazer tailored by some master. They were so to-be-noticed that there was something almost theatrical about their entrance.

"Two very dry martinis on the rocks," Quist told Willard

as they sat down at their table, "and as I remember, Caroline, a frozen daiquiri."

"You do remember," Caroline said. She looked around the crowded garden. "What fun!" Her voice was cultivated, but without affectation. "I rarely go anywhere for lunch any more. Mark is never available. I think some of these people remember me from the old days."

"Old days my foot," Quist said. "They're looking at you because you're quite fabulous."

"Thank you, sir," Caroline said. "I thought you two had forgotten me. I never see you."

"It's a busy time," Quist said, "and we don't circulate in the world of The Beautiful People."

"Why should you? You two *are* beautiful people. Are you still in love?"

"I just keep Lydia around because she writes good copy," Quist said.

"I just put up with Julian because he's my boss," Lydia said.

"How lucky you both have everything for each other," Caroline said.

The waiter brought their drinks. They toasted each other silently and sipped. Quist glanced at the menu the waiter handed him. "Lobster Newburg is a specialty of the house," he said. "A fresh green salad and gluten toast?"

"It sounds marvelous." Caroline put down her glass as the waiter left. "It doesn't dilute my pleasure any, Julian, to know that you and Lydia don't take the lunch hour of a busy day just to say hello to an old friend. What can Mark and I do for you?"

Quist laughed. "You're a very sharp chick," he said.

"But I love you both," Caroline said. He drank a little

of his martini, and then he laid it on the line without any trimmings or sales talk. Caroline listened, smiling.

"It's very tempting," she said, when he'd finished, "but I think I have to say 'no.' "

"Tempting?" Quist said.

"Marilyn Martin's clothes are marvelous," Caroline said. "It would be a delight to have a whole new wardrobe of her things. I guess I miss the old days a little, being a public glamor girl. I'm not without vanity, Julian. It would be fun, and I'd like to do you a favor. But—no."

Lydia looked at Quist. "Almost your very words, Julian," she said.

"Why 'no'?"

"I couldn't go all the places you'd like me to go," Caroline said, "because of Mark. He doesn't like society gatherings and first nights. And he's too busy. When he wants to go to London, I go; when he wants to go anywhere else on business, I go. I couldn't follow any routine you set up for me."

"It wouldn't be that rigid, Caroline," Quist said. "You go to London, we simply arrange to have you seen there, photographed there. We follow you. When you're free, we might suggest things to do or places to go. You wouldn't in any way be a slave to our whims."

"Still—no, Julian." Caroline's smile suggested it was hiding some inner unhappiness. "There wouldn't be enough times I could appear in public with Mark to do you much good. And I have my pride, darling. I wouldn't like to suddenly be everywhere without a man. It wouldn't be very glamorous."

"We could provide you with an escort," Lydia said.

Caroline laughed. "Mark might not like that—I hope!"

"Why don't we ask him?" Quist said. "Lay a little stress on your doing me a favor. But there is something else."

"Oh?"

"Marilyn Martin would, I think, pay you ten thousand dollars to undertake this adventure for six months. It would be a job—strictly business."

Caroline looked at him, her lips slightly parted. "Ten thousand dollars?"

"The price of that ring you're wearing on your left hand," Quist said. "But it would be pocket money you wouldn't have to ask for."

"You devil!" Caroline said. "How did you know I'd like that?"

"If you were mine," Quist said, "I'd want to keep some kind of collar and chain on you. Purse strings, maybe? But let's talk to Mark. It might be useful to him, be an indirect but plus publicity for Stillwell Enterprises. May I put it to him?"

Anything for a client, Quist thought.

He was sitting naked, except for a towel around his middle, in the steam at the Athletic Club, sweat oozing out of every pore in his body. Scarcely visible in the steamy fog, sitting at the other end of a wooden bench, was Mark Stillwell.

"Too rushed to have a social lunch, old boy," Mark had told Quist on the phone. "But if you'd care to join me for a workout and a sandwich at the club—"

To work under his kind of pressure, Mark explained, when Quist met him at the club and was taken up to the locker room that adjoined the gym, the swimming pool, and the squash courts, one had to stay fit.

14

"I'd rather miss a date with the most beautiful woman in the world—who happens to be my wife—than one of these workouts, Quist. Sound body leads to a sound mind and sound thinking."

Quist wondered if Mark had gotten his training as a cub scout leader. "A preoccupied dreamboat," Lydia had called him. No doubt about the fact of his good looks. Good body without an ounce of fat, muscles toned, square jaw, firm mouth, a little gray at the temples of his black head of hair, making him a perfect model for the businessman of distinction—dark, intense eyes that fixed on whoever he was with, as if to impress with the fact that listening was an art.

In the gym Mark went through a series of carefully programmed knee bends, toe touchings, workouts on the weight machines. In the pool he swam four laps. Quist watched, doing a few chin-ups on the big bar, swimming one leisurely lap while Mark did his four. Then to the steam room, and then to the needle-sharp showers, first hot, then cold. Then to the rubbing tables where two burly masseurs kneaded and pounded and caressed their bodies. At last to the sunlight room. They stretched out on two tables, an attendant covered their eyes with black patches, and the sun lamps came on.

"Five minutes of this," Mark said. "Can you talk now, old boy?"

Quist felt that if someone put an apple in his mouth, he could be served up for lunch. He talked, unable to see his listener or how he reacted. He unfolded Marilyn's ideas for Caroline, he mentioned the ten-thousand-dollar fee, he explained that it needn't interfere with their lives in any demanding fashion.

An alarm bell rang. The five minutes of sunburning was over. The lights went off. The attendant removed the black eye patches.

"God, I feel marvelous," Mark said.

He led the way to a room where a number of men sat at small tables, draped only in towels, looking tanned and, Quist thought, exhausted. An attendant approached.

"The usual," Mark said. He smiled, showing very white teeth. "Most of these poor devils work out, and then follow it up with two or three martinis. Whole thing wasted. I take a glass of buttermilk with some rye crisps. Have whatever you like, of course, old boy."

"Dancing girls?" Quist suggested.

That, Mark said, was a very funny idea. But seriously—

Seriously, Quist thought, a Bloody Mary would be just fine.

"It's an interesting proposition," Mark said at last. Quist was glad to know he'd been listening. "You've talked to Caroline, of course?"

"She said 'no,' but she said I could talk to you."

"Wonderful girl," Mark said. "Always thinks of me first. Who could ask for more?"

"Not even the King of Siam," Quist said. "I think the idea amused and tempted her. But, as you say, you come first."

The attendant brought buttermilk, rye crisps, and a Bloody Mary.

"A good deal of the time I'm a selfish person," Mark said, frowning at the buttermilk. "Oh, Caroline has every-thing she could ask for—clothes, jewels, cars, homes. But I don't give her as much of my time as she might want. Can't. Running Stillwell Enterprises is a thirty-six-hour-a-day job. What I mean is, there aren't enough hours in the day. I sometimes think Caroline misses a more active social life. Before we were married, she was—well, enormously popular in her circle of friends. Stage and screen people."

"Without half trying," Quist said.

"But, as I said, yours is an interesting proposition." The dark eyes fixed on Quist. "Can I trust you with something completely confidential?"

"If you don't know the answer to that, don't tell me," Quist said.

"I do trust you," Mark said. He drew a deep breath. "I am one of three men being considered to head up one of the biggest business mergers of all time. The people who will make the decision are in the upper echelons in society. They go to all the 'right places,' rub elbows with all the people who 'make news.' If there is one thing against my chances—and they've told me this—I haven't made myself well enough known to the public. My business has always been a very private operation."

Quist smiled. "What you need is a public relations expert."

"So I've been told," Mark said. "But I don't like that sort of thing. It would be phony—not me. However—"

"If Caroline came back into the public eye, without seeming to push; if she began to appear in those 'right places' and was seen with the people who 'make news'—"

"Exactly," Mark said. "If it was handled with taste."

"Can you imagine Caroline doing anything that was tasteless?"

"Certainly not."

"Her charm, her beauty, would also make you glamorous," Quist said. "We wouldn't be promoting Caroline Cummings, the former movie star. It would be 'Mrs. Mark Stillwell, charming wife of Mark Stillwell, one of the nation's financial geniuses.' "

Mark frowned. "But tacked onto it would be the fact that she was wearing a Marilyn Martin creation. Wouldn't it presently become pretty obvious?"

"My dear Mark, we wouldn't handle it with a sledge hammer. No comments in the regular press. *Women's Wear Daily* would dig out the fact that Caroline's clothes were designed by Marilyn. That's their business. They tell the same facts about Mrs. Paley, Mrs. Ford, Mrs. Onassis. We'd never mention it in our press releases. She was there, she was seen, and a hundred thousand women will be digging to find out where she gets her clothes. It will happen without our lifting a finger, except to get her to those 'right places.' "

"It could do me some good, don't you think?" Mark asked.

"Being married to Caroline would do anyone some good," Quist said.

Mark nodded. "I think I buy it," he said. He reached for his buttermilk.

"There is one drawback," Quist said. Mark withdrew from his buttermilk. "Unless you are prepared to change your life style, Mark, Caroline will have to go to a lot of these 'right places' without you."

"I see that. And I simply couldn't be available all the time."

"Caroline can't go wandering around without some kind of escort," Quist said. "A glamorous wallflower isn't quite the answer. I can think of a hundred men who'd like to take her places, but she felt you might object. In all honesty, it might make for gossip that wouldn't help you."

There was a long silence while Mark fiddled with a rye crisp without eating it.

"There is my brother," Mark said finally.

"I didn't know you had a brother."

"Jerome—Jerry. He lives with us. I mean, he lives in our Westchester house. He has a studio there."

"Studio?"

"He's a painter—an artist of sorts," Mark said. "Jerry was a late child, very much a mother's boy. He just never had what it takes to make it in a competitive world." His mouth moved slightly in what Quist guessed was meant to be a smile. "He's quite attractive—pictorially."

"Meaning?"

"We're talking about being photographed, aren't we—being attractive in public, aren't we?"

Quist decided he wanted to get dressed and go home, but he didn't move.

"Jerry wears clothes well—the most casual kind of clothes," Mark said. "He rides a horse well. He plays a first-rate golf and a very fair tennis. Pictorially he should fit the bill." He seemed to relish the word. It implied a kind of contempt for his brother except for externals.

Quist thought later, too much later, that he should have obeyed the impulse he had to drop the whole thing right then.

"Is he a good painter?" he asked.

"Jerry?" Mark said from far away somewhere.

"We were talking about him," Quist said, sounding sharp.

Mark shrugged. "I'm not qualified to answer that artistically," he said. "Financially, he doesn't do well. Jerry will do what I ask him in the matter of Caroline's need for an escort. He has to do what I ask him because he's dependent on me."

"How do he and Caroline get along?"

"She likes him," Mark said, as though it was an astonishing fact.

"And he?"

"My dear old boy, do you know anyone who doesn't like Caroline? Would you like to meet Jerry, talk to him about this? I can have him in your office any time you say tomorrow."

Quist took a swallow of his Bloody Mary and wished it was a double. "If you buy the idea, I think I'd like to talk to Caroline and your brother together."

"Oh, I buy the idea," Mark said. "The more I think about it, the more good I think it might do me."

Late that afternoon, sitting on the terrace of his duplex apartment on Beekman Place, overlooking the East River, with Lydia, Quist told her about his athletic noon hour with Mark Stillwell.

"He may, as you said this morning, be a preoccupied dreamboat, love, but his preoccupation is, I think, entirely with himself. I hadn't noticed it before, but—if you'll forgive a four-letter word—I think our Mark is a bit of a prick."

Lydia smiled at him. "There are five letters in that word, darling," she said.

The plan to launch Marilyn Martin's glamor clothes for mature women got under way the next day, after Quist had seen Caroline and Jerry Stillwell in his office.

It wouldn't be quite accurate to say that Quist found Jerry Stillwell unexpectedly attractive—the unexpected part of it. The put-down given his younger brother by Mark Stillwell had prepared Quist to find Jerry blessed with a degree of charm. He was about six feet tall, just a little shorter than Quist. He had brownish hair, bleached a little by the summer sun, and a healthy tan. His eyes were a bright blue, with tiny lines at their corners. He looked like a man who smiled easily. That summer morning he wore a navy-blue sport shirt, tieless, a seersucker jacket, a little wrinkled, and a faded pair of tan slacks. Nothing stylish; yet when he moved, there was a suggestion of elegance.

"It's asking too much of Jerry," Caroline said, first thing. "It will take too much time away from his work, his painting. I couldn't ask him to give that much."

"If you asked me, I would give it happily," Jerry said. "As it is, Mark has told me. I may not be quite so happy about that. But you know, Caroline, being with you, when I'm needed, will be a delight."

"Let's get this all quite clear," Quist said. "You're not being asked to do anyone a favor, Jerry. This is a business proposition. Caroline is to get ten thousand dollars for carrying on for six months. You will get five. Caroline will have to spend a lot more time at it than you—clothes fittings, endless details about accessories, and the like. Marilyn Martin wants something, and she's prepared to pay for it."

"Five thousand dollars!" Jerry said. "I could go to Paris when this is over. I could live in Paris for a year on five thousand." He grinned at Caroline. "Please, Sis, *let* me do it!"

Quist was asked, much later, if he thought there was "anything" between Caroline and her brother-in-law. "Rapport" was too complex a word to give a cop. They seemed to get along without tensions of any sort. Tensions between

21

a man and a woman can include desire, jealousy, hunger frustrated by some sort of moral code. There seemed to be a complete relaxation between these two people. They liked each other, felt a mutual respect, but there were no hidden fires. That's what Quist felt that morning, and much later when he was asked.

It took about a month for "project Stillwell" to get under way. In that month Marilyn Martin designed and made clothes for Caroline. Caroline made herself available for endless fittings and consultations. Quist almost forgot about the program, up to his neck in a dozen other promotions. Bobby Hilliard, one of his best people, looking like a shy young Jimmy Stewart, along with Lydia, was to plan Caroline's campaign.

Finally the time came for what Marilyn Martin called a "dry run." There was to be a weekend party at the Stillwells' Westchester estate. The house party itself would be smallish; there'd be people in and out who lived in the area. Quist, Lydia, and Bobby Hilliard were invited, along with Marilyn, of course. During the weekend Caroline would wear some of the clothes that had been made for her. Marilyn wanted the reactions of the people who would be there, particularly the women, without their knowing that anything special was in the wind.

Quist and Lydia arrived in his cream-colored Mercedes about cocktail time on Friday afternoon. Bobby Hilliard was due to arrive with Marilyn in time for dinner.

Quist was changing into a dark blue tropical worsted suit when Mark Stillwell knocked on his door. Mark looked worried.

"Something a little unexpected has happened," he said.
"Oh?"

"Quite out of the blue," Mark said. "About an hour ago I had a phone call from David Isham Lewis. You know who he is?"

A power house in the financial world, Quist knew.

"He is one of the men I told you about—looking me over to head up that business merger. Extremely important to me. I think this is a kind of trap, a kind of a test."

"In what way?"

"He called. He and Marcia, his wife, had planned to spend the weekend at the Belleair Club. Something unsatisfactory about the accommodations. He wondered if they might 'camp out' in one of our guest rooms. I told him we had a small house party. He wouldn't dream of barging in. Of course I insisted. I think he meant to catch me off guard, to see me in circumstances in which I was unprepared for him. I don't mind that, you understand. I have no secrets. Except—"

"Except Caroline's deal with Marilyn?"

"Yes."

"Well, take it easy, Mark. None of us wants it known, either. It would spoil the whole future program." Quist smiled. "We won't let you down, Mark. We all know what fork to use."

"Oh, I wasn't worried about that, old boy. But this weekend becomes much more important to me than it was. I'd appreciate it if you'd keep an eye on Lewis. You may, as a disinterested observer, be able to tell better how he's reacting than I can."

The next few hours were like being introduced to the cast of characters in a play—a play which none of them knew wasn't going to be produced. Caroline and Lydia looked stunning. Mark, a little flushed, seemed a trifle overeager. Jerry Stillwell seemed relaxed, at ease. The new faces for Quist included David Isham Lewis. He was a big man, in his fifties, square-jawed, diamond-bright blue eyes, bushy dark eyebrows and thick white hair. He had power written all over him. His wife Marcia, probably fifteen years younger, blond, looked washed out for her age, worried, uncomfortable in this setting.

There was a young man named Patrick Grant who looked like a professional athlete and talked to Lewis like a business computer, who turned out to be Mark's executive secretary. He was a little flashy and had an eye for the ladies, particularly, Quist noted, for Lydia, whom he was seeing for the first time.

Perhaps the most interesting member of the household —interesting because Quist couldn't quite place her—was a Mrs. Beatrice Lorimer. She was introduced as Mark's aunt, but she must have been a very much younger sister of Mark's father or mother. She looked Mark's age and was probably not more than five years older. She was beautifully turned out, cultivated, and had, Quist found out as the evening wore on, a nice sense of humor. She played with skill the game of flirting with the men, but underneath her pleasant façade Quist sensed unusual strength and perhaps just a touch of cruelty.

From outside came a young man, a neighbor, named Tommy Bayne, who played the piano beautifully and sang a whole collection of the late Noel Coward's songs. With him was his fiancée Miriam Talbot, whom Quist referred to later—to Lydia—as "that topless tootsie," who seemed very much more interested in Mark, to Mark's embarrassment, than in young Mr. Bayne.

There were cocktails and then a magnificent buffet sup-

24

per, presided over and skillfully served by a houseman in a white jacket named Shallert. There must have been a corp of other servants, but none of them appeared.

Marilyn and Bobby appeared in time for supper and the cast was complete. It was all very gay in a dull way, Quist thought later. Young Mr. Bayne played and played, and Miriam Talbot flirted with Mark, and everyone but Mark and David Isham Lewis drank a little too much—a sort of self-protective mechanism. The ladies admired Caroline's dress—close-fitting, much bare shoulder, and a slit up one side of the fullish skirt that revealed a beautiful leg up to there! Marilyn was pleased and took to her bed early. Young Mr. Bayne and his Miss Talbot didn't seem to know when to go home, and when they finally did, a little after one, the evening broke up.

Quist went to his room, undressed, and put on his white terry-cloth robe and a pair of sandals. He opened the door to his room, looked up and down the empty hall, and then let himself into the adjoining room.

Lydia was sitting at the dressing table, wearing a very short and revealing little white thing, brushing her long black hair. She turned her head and said "Hi, darling," as if she'd been expecting Quist.

He said "Hi" and stretched out on her bed, hands behind his head. "I guess one would say it went well," he said.

"If you're talking about Caroline's dress, it went beautifully," Lydia said. "She was much admired by the ladies, which is the name of the game. I thought the men salivated a little, too."

"Not Mr. Patrick Grant," Quist said.

Lydia laughed that special kind of laugh women have when they hear the sound of jealousy in their man's voice, and have a clear conscience. "Mr. Grant imagines that the ladies would forget Burt Reynolds if he could just get his picture on the center fold of *Cosmopolitan,*" she said. She smiled at Quist. "He invited himself to my room, and when I refused demurely, he invited me to his."

"Am I in the way?" Quist asked.

"Idiot." Lydia brushed for a moment, looking at herself with pleasure in the mirror. She had everything she wanted, which did not include Mr. Patrick Grant. He did have a very nice body, and very white teeth, and very exploratory dark eyes, but she didn't want him. "You seemed quite taken with Aunt Beatrice," she said.

"Aunt Beatrice is quite a gal," Quist said, looking up at the ceiling as though he saw pictures there. "She knows something that is unhappily out of date—excepting present company. She knows how to create a sense of mystery about herself, both sexual and intellectual."

"Am I mysterious, darling?" Lydia asked.

Quist turned his head. "I have examined every inch of you, from top to toe, love, and I always feel I've missed something. It's your special magic, of course, which you keep very much to yourself."

"Thank you, sir."

"Beatrice Lorimer has the same gift. The more you talk to her, the more you want to find out what it is she is protecting with her chic, her wit, her worldliness. You know all there is to know about most women today after ten minutes. Their clothes reveal everything there is to see, and their conversation reveals that there is nothing between their ears. There are deep wells in you, darling, and in Beatrice Lorimer, that beg to be explored."

"Would you like to explore Aunt Beatrice?"

26

"I would and I will," Quist said, "but not in bed. What did you think of the great Mr. Lewis?"

"He beats his wife," Lydia said matter-of-factly.

"I wondered."

"I'm quite serious," Lydia said. "All those scarfs and things that flutter around her. They hide bruises. I spotted a couple."

"Don't feel too sorry for her," Quist said. "Most masochists marry sadists by choice. They cherish their bruises. What about young Mr. Bayne, the road company Noel Coward?"

"Eye on the main chance," Lydia said. "Which I would say does not include his girl friend Miriam."

"Miriam belongs to what the French call *les hotsies,*" Quist said. "She also is a main chancer. Mark was the richest man there except your wife beater."

Lydia sighed contentedly. "They are all so dull compared to us, darling."

"You are a vain creature," Quist said.

"Having you for my man has turned my head."

Quist swung up into a sitting position. "Before you turn me into a sex maniac, I suggest a swim in the pool," he said. "It's a warm, beautiful, moonlight night."

"I've just done my hair, Julian!"

"Bathing cap."

"I don't have one."

"In the bathhouse."

"I don't have a suit. You really want to swim?"

"It would be a nice buildup to a big moment," he said.

And so they went out to the pool together. The rest of the household appeared to be bedded down for the night. They splashed about in the pool, touching now and then, pleased and happy with each other.

And then Quist went to get himself a cigar. That was when the big moment came, but not the one he had anticipated. That was when he found Caroline, very dead, behind the lilac bushes.

chapter 2

Perhaps it was imagination, but it seemed to Quist that the moonlight had suddenly cast a chill over the night. He stood where he was, watching Lydia go into the house. He was glad she hadn't had to look at what was behind the lilac bushes. Caroline had changed out of Marilyn Martin's sensational evening dress. She had come out—or been brought out—into the pool area wearing a pale green voile dressing gown. The robe had been ripped open, revealing a black lace bra and black lace panties and a pair of satin bedrooms slippers, stained by the dew-wet grass. The bra had been torn away and her whole body stabbed, slashed at, obscenely destroyed. It was the work of some kind of monster. One of the stab wounds must have killed her almost instantly. Her mouth gaped open in a silent scream, her eyes wide, staring blindly at the moon.

Quist had noticed that she was wearing bedroom slippers.

He didn't go back to look at her again. He hoped he would never have to see her again as he had found her. He also didn't want to confuse any kind of clues the soft earth and the dew-soaked grass might hold for the police.

His cigar tasted like rope. He started to throw it away, changed his mind, buried the hot end for a moment in the earth at his feet, and when it was out, dropped it into his dressing gown pocket. He wondered how long it would be before there would be a response to the call Lydia must have made by now. There might very well be a State Police car patrolling this area of very rich homes, and if there was, the response should be quick.

Even as he thought about it, he heard the wail of a siren, coming closer and closer. Down across the wide expanse of lawn he saw car lights turning in at the gate—headlights and the red blinkers on the top of the car. A trooper came running down toward the pool. Lydia had evidently told them where the action was.

Quist stood perfectly still until the trooper, a dark young man with a hard face, reached him. His hand rested on the butt of a holstered gun.

"We had a call," he said. "A homicide reported. A woman called."

"My name is Quist. A Miss Morton and I were swimming in the pool. I came out of the water to get myself a cigar and I found her—over there back of that bush. I sent Miss Morton to phone you."

The trooper walked over to the lilac bushes. He looked down. "Jesus Christ!" he said. He turned back to Quist. "Who is she?"

"Mrs. Mark Stillwell," Quist said.

"Stillwell's wife?"

"Yes."

"Stay where you are," the trooper said. "I've got to check in." He took it on the run back to his car, where the red lights still blinked off and on.

It seemed to take forever, but finally the trooper came back. He seemed not to want to look at the body again. "There's a crazy jalopy parked down by the gate, painted half a dozen colors. You know who it belongs to?"

"No."

The trooper took a notebook out of his pocket. "So let's have it, Mister. You say your name is Quist?"

"Julian Quist. Miss Morton and I are house guests for the weekend. We came out here a little before two o'clock for a swim before going to bed."

"Just you two?"

"Yes. I'd left my robe over that chair. I came out of the water to get myself a cigar and I saw Mrs. Stillwell's hand —like it is now."

"No one else but you two?"

"I've told you."

"You didn't see or hear anyone else?"

"No one, nothing. It must have happened before we came out here." Quist saw that several lights had popped on in the house.

"You didn't notice her when you came down here to swim?"

"No."

"How come there's no one here now but you? Where's her husband?"

"I told Miss Morton not to spread an alarm until you got here," Quist said. "I thought you wouldn't want the place tramped over till you'd had a chance at it. It looks as though your siren has people stirring now."

"Who's up there?"

Quist listed them: Mark and Jerry Stillwell, Mrs. Lorimer, Patrick Grant, Lydia, the David Isham Lewises, Bobby Hilliard and Marilyn Martin, Shallert and other servants.

"Who owns the jalopy?" the trooper asked.

"No idea," Quist said. "This isn't jalopy country."

"You haven't left anyone out?"

"There were two other guests earlier in the evening; a man named Tommy Bayne, a girl named Miriam Talbot. They went home about one o'clock."

"I know Bayne," the trooper said. "He has a cottage about three miles down the road."

"As soon as Bayne and his girl left, the evening broke up. Everyone went to bed. Miss Morton and I didn't feel like sleeping. We came down here for a swim."

"Motive," the trooper said. "Why would anyone do this?"

"No idea, not even a guess," Quist said.

"I have an idea I saw that jalopy earlier tonight," the trooper said, worrying at it. "On patrol I think I saw it outside the Boat Club."

"I don't know this part of the world," Quist said. "What's the Boat Club?"

"Crummy beer joint not too far from the village. Hangout for hippies, long hairs, creeps, pot smokers. We've tried to close it up for some time, but someone has political pull somewhere. If some of those jerks are wandering around here, we may have a quick answer. They'd knock off their own mothers to get the bread for a fix. Has to be some kind of a lunatic who'd carve her up like that."

32

An understatement, Quist thought. "Can I ask what your name is, Trooper?"

"Sergeant Pollet."

"I'd like to get on some clothes, Sergeant."

"You'd better wait here till Lieutenant Sims shows up," Pollet said. "He'll be in charge."

The private moment, the quiet moment, was over. Mass confusion and horror was on the way. Quist saw Mark Stillwell running down from the house, followed by Patrick Grant and Lydia. Lydia was carrying some kind of bundle.

Mark Stillwell's face was chalk-white. "Where is she?" he asked, breathless, his voice hoarse.

"Maybe you better not see her just yet, Mr. Stillwell. Not till Lieutenant Sims has had a chance to look over the ground." There was respect in Pollet's voice that hadn't been there for Quist.

"Don't be a goddamn fool, Pollet! Where is she?" Mark demanded. He looked around. He saw the white hand behind the lilac bush. He broke away from Pollet's restraining hand and ran to it. He bent down. A cry split the pale night—the cry of a wounded animal.

Patrick Grant was at Quist's side. He looked stunned and a little groggy, as if he'd just been awakened.

"No doubt?" he asked. "It is Caroline?"

"No doubt."

Another agonized cry from behind the flower bed sent shivers down Quist's spine. Lydia, wearing slacks and a yellow sweater, handed him the bundle.

"Clothes," she said. "The bathhouse."

She must have known he was feeling naked. Pollet was trying to get Mark away from the body and so there was no one to stop Quist from going into the bathhouse. Lydia had brought him exactly what he would have asked for: socks, underwear, a pair of calfskin loafers, flannel slacks, a green knitted sports shirt, a corduroy jacket. As he pulled on the slacks, he heard a second siren coming up the drive. Then it stopped some distance away, and he heard voices shouting.

Quist got into his jacket. Lydia—bless her—had even put his wallet in his inside pocket. He transferred his cigar case and lighter from the robe he'd been wearing, and went out once more to the pool. Just as he got there, two troopers came across the lawn, dragging a third person between them. It took Quist a moment to make certain that it was a man, not a woman. Reddish brown hair hung well down below the shoulders; blue Levis and a blue workshirt; stained sneakers on the feet. But definitely a boy, probably still in his teens.

"Looks like we got him!" Lieutenant Sims said. He had close-cropped gray hair, a tanned, hard face, gimlet black eyes. "Sonofabitch was hiding in the shrubbery halfway up the drive. Knife on him. What's your name, kid?"

The boy looked frightened but defiant. "Johnny Tiptoe," he said.

"Play games with me and you'll wish you hadn't," Sims said. "What's your name?"

"Johnny Tiptoe."

"What the hell kind of a name is that?"

"I know him, Lieutenant," the other trooper said. "He's a country music singer. Works the Boat Club now and then. They call him Johnny Tiptoe."

"What's your real name, kid?" Sims asked.

"Johnny Tiptoe," the boy said. "Look, I don't know

what the hell's going on here, man. I split from the Boat Club about two o'clock. Ran out of gas right in front of this pad. I saw lights. I figured in a place like this there'd be cars and a chauffeur and probably gas. I walked in, looking for help, and all of a sudden a siren job came up the driveway. I panicked and hid. I figured I'd tripped some kind of alarm."

"Hand over that knife, boy," Sims said. "You always carry this?"

"I carry it."

Sims turned a flashlight on it. "Looks like it was cleaned off by shoving it in the ground," he said. He handed it to the other trooper. "Have the lab go over it. There may still be traces of blood on it."

"This is a gas, man," Johnny Tiptoe said. "Why should there be blood on it?"

"Because you killed a woman with it," Sims said.

"You've blown your mind, man! I haven't seen any woman—till you brought me here now."

Pollet came back from the flower bed with a weeping Mark Stillwell leaning heavily on him. Sims, with Patrick Grant behind him, went over to the lilac bushes to have a look. Quist heard a sharp cry from Grant.

Sims came back to where Mark was still clinging to Pollet. "It's a pretty bad scene for you, Mr. Stillwell," he said. "It may not help much to know that I think we've nailed the creep who did it." His black eyes burned into Johnny Tiptoe. "This character was probably looking for something to steal in the bathhouse when your wife discovered him. Killing is second nature to his kind."

"No way, man!" Johnny Tiptoe said.

"If the boy didn't leave the Boat Club until two o'clock,"

Quist said in a quiet voice, "—and he should be able to prove that if he's telling the truth—he couldn't have killed Mrs. Stillwell."

"Who are you?" Sims said.

"His name is Julian Quist," Pollet said. "He was swimming down here with Miss Morton over there. He found the body."

"We came down here about quarter to two," Quist said. "I found Mrs. Stillwell about two-thirty. It happened before a quarter to two, because nothing happened while we were here."

"Those kids at the Boat Club would lie themselves to death for this guy," Sims said.

More people were spewing out of the house and coming down across the lawn toward the pool. Quist saw David Isham Lewis and his wife, and Marilyn, and Bobby Hilliard, the boyish Jimmy Stewart. Standing on the terrace in front of the house, but making no move to come down to the pool, was Beatrice Lorimer. Almost everyone seemed to have thrown on the first clothes that came to hand. Beatrice Lorimer looked immaculately prepared. The proper clothes for a crisis.

Bobby Hilliard and Marilyn joined Quist.

"The ball game is over," Quist said to Marilyn. "Caroline won't wear any more clothes for you, Marilyn."

Marilyn appeared to be in shock.

Lieutenant Sims was demanding attention. "I would like all of you to go back to the house," he said. "We need time to go over the ground here, without having any clues obliterated by careless walking around."

"I must stay with her," Mark said in a broken voice.

36

"But stay where I tell you, Mr. Stillwell," Sims said. "The rest of you, back to the house, please. Wait for us there. I'll need to get a statement from each one of you. It's just routine, because I think we've got it nailed down." His eyes blazed at Johnny Tiptoe, who was still in the grip of the other trooper.

The guests began to drift back toward the house, where Beatrice Lorimer waited, like a sentinel, on the terrace. Quist, Lydia, Marilyn, and Bobby Hilliard were grouped together. Quist could feel Marilyn's fingernails biting into his arm. He spoke to Hilliard.

"We seem to be trusted, Bobby. No escort."

"So?"

"Somewhere down the driveway is Johnny Tiptoe's jalopy," Quist said. "Think you could slide around the back of the house and take a look at it?"

"I could try," Bobby said.

"See how much gas there is in his tank," Quist said. "Watch your step. There'll be more troopers coming."

"You don't believe the boy did it?" Lydia asked.

"If he did, he could have been miles away from here, even if he had to walk," Quist said. "We were in that pool for forty-five minutes, love, before I found her. He had that much time if he did it. Why would he hang around?"

"Some kind of a nut, fascinated by his own handiwork," Bobby said.

"Maybe. Maybe he's telling the truth. He makes it miraculously easy for Sims and company."

"Why do you care, Julian?" Marilyn asked in a dead voice.

Quist's face looked rock-hard. "Caroline was my friend,"

he said. "I want to be sure the right sonofabitch burns for this!"

The Lewises and Patrick Grant reached the house ahead of them, but Beatrice Lorimer still waited on the terrace. Not a hair was out of place. If she had taken off her make-up before going to bed, there had been time for her to reapply it, skillfully. She was wearing a tweed skirt, a man's shirt with an orange scarf at her throat, and sturdy-looking walking shoes.

"There's no question about it, Quist?" she asked in a flat voice. "It is Caroline?"

"No question," Quist said.

"How awful for you and Miss Morton," Mrs. Lorimer said.

Quist looked as if he hadn't heard her correctly. "Just a shade more awful for Caroline," he said.

"Do they have any leads at all?" Mrs. Lorimer asked.

"They've arrested a young hippie singer they found hanging around on the grounds," Quist said. "The trooper, I think, would like to think it's another Manson case."

"Thank God!" Beatrice Lorimer said.

"Thank God for what?" Quist asked.

"One's first thought has to be that it was someone in this household," she said. "How is Mark taking it?"

"He is properly shattered," Quist said. Out of the corner of his eye he saw Bobby Hilliard drift into the house. He felt Lydia's cool fingers touch his hand. She sensed that he was suddenly angered by Beatrice Lorimer's lack of feeling for Caroline. Her touch warned him not to explode. Beatrice Lorimer was behaving more like a spectator at a bull-fight than someone who had just lost a loved member of the family. Quist put a reassuring hand on Lydia's shoulder.

"Shallert is preparing coffee and sandwiches," Beatrice Lorimer said. "We might as well prepare ourselves for a long haul."

They walked through the French windows that opened from the terrace into the great entrance hall of the house. Quist saw David Lewis talking on a telephone, his frightened wife hovering a few yards away. A beautiful Wyeth painting hung over Lewis's head, calm in an atmosphere of tension. The first thing a great tycoon does when there is trouble, Quist thought, is call his lawyer. Or perhaps the murder of the wife of a brother tycoon might do something to the stock market. Lewis had still another explanation as he put down the phone and joined Quist and Lydia. Marilyn, like Bobby, had disappeared somewhere.

"I was calling the top brass in the State Police," Lewis said. "They'll be sending someone from their detective division. I want a good, discreet man. If this is bungled, the media will turn it into a Roman holiday."

"You'll almost certainly get your name in the paper," Quist said.

"But thank God they caught that boy," Lewis said. "It's wrapped up before it can be blown out of proportion."

"If he did it," Quist said.

Lewis's bushy black eyebrows moved upward. "You have any doubts, Quist?"

"I should have been named Thomas," Quist said. "I always doubt until I know for sure."

The layout in the dining room wasn't quite believable. There were two Silex pots of coffee, steaming hot; exquisite china; stacks of sandwiches surrounded by bowls of olives, pickles, and relishes. Everything looked as if it had been prepared long in advance, which, of course, it could have been. Extraordinary backstage efficiency, Quist thought. The shaded wall brackets gave the room a soft glow. It kept worn, tense faces from looking too bleak. Beatrice Lorimer presided over the coffeepots. She had obviously succeeded to the role of hostess.

Marcia Lewis, scarfs covering what Lydia insisted were bruises, talked a little hysterically.

"Caroline took us to our room when the party broke up," she said. "To make sure we had everything we needed. She seemed so relaxed and sure of herself. She was such a lovely person. Why do you suppose she went to the pool at that time of night?"

"Pools are made to swim in, my dear," Lewis said. "Mr. Quist and Miss Morton had the same impulse—later. Unhappily for Caroline that boy was lying in wait for someone."

Lydia moved Quist toward the far end of the room. "She didn't go down there to swim, Julian."

"What makes you think not?"

"She wouldn't be wearing a black lace bra and black lace panties if she was going swimming, Julian. She'd have had on a bathing suit or nothing under her robe."

"Planned to dress in the bathhouse?"

"Those undies were what she wore under her evening dress," Lydia said. "She wouldn't have tossed them around down in the bathhouse. She'd have worn something else— or nothing—if she planned to swim. And she'd never have worn those slippers—unless she went out in a great hurry. Some kind of pressure."

"Maybe she spotted someone out on the grounds and went down to investigate."

"With Shallert and a houseful of servants to go?"

"Maybe she went to meet a lover," Quist said. "That might explain the fancy pants."

"Not Caroline."

"How do you know?"

"I just know," Lydia said. "Unless Mark was going to meet her there. Where was Mark when she went down there?"

"He'll tell us sooner or later," Quist said.

Bobby Hilliard appeared in the far doorway and came toward them. "No gas," he said. "Bone-dry."

"Good boy," Quist said.

"There are more cops now, dozens of them," Bobby said. "I only just got away with it. They're towing the jalopy away now."

"So at least part of Johnny Tiptoe's story holds up," Quist said.

It was at least an hour before Lieutenant Sims came up from the pool. There was a stranger with him, a rather nice-looking sandy-haired man in civilian clothes. Mark had evidently stayed behind, or been allowed to ride with the body to the county morgue. Everyone was asked to assemble in the living room, and it was the sandy-haired man who seemed to be in charge.

"I'm Captain Jadwin of the detective division of the State Police," he said. "I'm not in charge of this investigation. Fortunately Lieutenant Sims has done a first-rate job before I got here. The Tiptoe boy seems to be our man. People at the Boat Club swear he didn't leave there till two o'clock, but they would lie for him, without question. However, his story about running out of gas is simply not true.

Lieutenant informs me that there was plenty of gas in his car."

Quist glanced at Bobby Hilliard. Bobby's Jimmy Stewart face was twisted into an almost comic look of disbelief. David Lewis was lighting a cigar, looking relaxed and content. They were setting up Johnny Tiptoe, Quist thought. Lewis did have pull!

Jadwin fished a cigarette out of his pocket, put it in his mouth, but didn't light it. It bobbed up and down as he spoke. He had, Quist saw, pleasant gray eyes that didn't miss much.

"Our job now is just to clear up a few loose ends," Jadwin said. "There was a party, I understand, but only two guests who didn't live here in the house—for the weekend, at least. When those two guests left, a little after one, the party broke up and people went to their rooms for the night."

"Not Mark—Mr. Stillwell—and I," Patrick Grant said. "We went to his study at the back of the house. We had work to do. We always have work to do."

"So Mr. Stillwell didn't go up to his wife's room with her?" Jadwin asked.

"No. She kissed him good night in the downstairs hallway and went upstairs to see that the Lewises had everything they needed. Mark and I went back to the study."

"At the back of the house, you say. You didn't have a view of the pool area from there?"

"No. But it is a warm night, Captain. The windows are all open. If Caroline had screamed, we'd have heard her."

"Miss Morton and I were up," Quist said. "There was no scream."

"I'm coming to you and Miss Morton, Mr. Quist," Jadwin said pleasantly. "But another question, Mr. Grant. When did you know something had gone wrong?"

"We heard the police siren coming up the drive."

"Miss Morton, I understand, had come back from the pool to call for help. You didn't see her or hear her?"

"No."

"She didn't come looking for you?"

"If she did, she didn't find us," Grant said.

Jadwin's gray eyes shifted. "Did you look for Mr. Stillwell, Miss Morton?"

"No. I called the police and then went up to my room to get some clothes," Lydia said.

"You didn't think Mr. Stillwell should be told what had happened to his wife?" Jadwin looked surprised.

"Julian—Mr. Quist—told me not to tell anyone."

Jadwin looked at Quist, and there was humor in his eyes. "I know something about you, Mr. Quist. We have a mutual friend, Lieutenant Kreevich of Manhattan's Homicide Squad. You were involved with him in the Sands case. The champagne killer they called him. You like to play detective."

"I thought it best for no one to be told till the police got here," Quist said. "I didn't think you'd want the place tramped over till you'd had a chance to see it."

"A quite sensible idea," Jadwin said. "You and Miss Morton were 'up,' you say?"

A little nerve twitched in Quist's cheek. "I went to Miss Morton's room after we'd gone upstairs."

"Oh?"

"Oh," Quist said. "We talked a while, and then we decided to go swimming. That was at about a quarter to two."

"We found your robe in the bathhouse," Jadwin said, "but no wet swim things, either yours or Miss Morton's."

"We swam, as the saying goes, in the raw," Quist said.

Jadwin glanced at Lydia and cleared his throat.

"When you went down to the pool, you didn't see Mrs. Stillwell's body?"

"No."

"But once you went in the pool, you were never out of sight of the area where it was found?"

"If you're asking if she could have been murdered while we were there, the answer is a positive no, Captain. After we'd been there for about three quarters of an hour, I went up out of the pool to get a cigar from the pocket of my robe."

"In the raw?"

"In the raw. I got a cigar and my lighter out of the robe. There was a gentle breeze blowing and I turned away from the pool to shield my lighter from it. That's how I happened to see Caroline's hand stretched out from behind the bush."

"And that was about two-thirty?"

"I wasn't wearing my watch," Quist said. "I'm guessing. But it wasn't more than six or seven minutes before Miss Morton called the State Police. They must have a record of the time."

Jadwin nodded. "Two-thirty-nine," he said. "You didn't see or hear anyone? This Tiptoe character, even by his own account, was wandering around the grounds at that time."

"I didn't see or hear anyone."

"You, Miss Morton? When you went up to the house?"

"No one."

"You dressed and came back down to the pool?"

44

"And brought Julian some clothes," Lydia said. "Sergeant Pollet was already there. The troopers responded very quickly."

"Pollet was on patrol, less than a mile away when they contacted him from the barracks."

"It's comforting, in this day and age, to find the police so readily available," David Lewis said, watching a smoke ring curl toward the ceiling.

Jadwin proceeded to get a short statement from everyone. The Lewises had gone to their room, where Caroline joined them for a few moments. Then to bed and nothing out of the ordinary till they heard the police siren.

Marilyn Martin had gone to bed earlier than anyone. She'd been almost too tired to sleep, so she'd taken a seconal pill. Nothing till the siren.

Bobby Hilliard had gone to his room, read for a little while, and then dozed off. The siren woke him. Jerry Stillwell, looking stunned, had much the same story.

And then Jadwin turned his mild gray attention to Beatrice Lorimer. Quist thought that this woman, certainly in her late forties, went quite a long way toward proving Marilyn Martin's point; there was a civilized glamor here that made the young girls of the day seem too obvious and too empty. Even her voice had a sexy quality to it.

"I think I may be the last person—with the exception of the Tiptoe boy—who saw Caroline alive," she said. "I was the last person to come upstairs. Believe it or not, I had debated the possibility of a swim. If I'd decided to go, it—it might have been me and not Caroline." She smiled a small, bitter smile. "It takes me rather longer to prepare myself to face the day than most younger women. A swim meant redoing my hair before breakfast. I decided against it. As I

45

reached the second floor, I saw Caroline come out of the Lewises' room. We chatted for a moment."

"About what, Mrs. Lorimer?"

Beatrice shrugged her elegant shoulders. "About the evening; about the party. About—about the dress she'd worn, which was, I must say, spectacular." She glanced at Marilyn. "About the next day and what was planned for it."

"What was planned for it?"

"Nothing too special. There's the pool, tennis courts, golf nearby. The guests would entertain themselves till late afternoon when, weather permitting, we were to have an outdoor barbecue at the pool."

"How did she seem?"

"Caroline? Her usual self. She is—was—a very relaxed, uncomplicated person. She was pleased with the way the evening had gone, barring perhaps a little too much of Tommy Bayne and his Noel Coward theme."

"Not distressed about anything?"

"No. She did say something to the effect that if Mark kept working at night, she might have to find herself a lover. It was a joke. I've never known a woman so involved with her husband as Caroline was." Beatrice drew a deep breath. "She loved him very much."

"She didn't suggest she might be going for a swim?"

"No. She wouldn't have gone by herself, I'm sure."

"But she did go down to the pool."

"I know. I can't guess why."

"She probably saw the Tiptoe boy and went to see what he was up to," Jadwin said.

"Are you saying she'd have gone to investigate a prowler by herself? With Mark and Patrick within call?"

"And yet she went," Jadwin said.

46

"The only explanation I can suggest, Captain, is that she saw someone down there she knew—one of us, a neighbor."

"None of you was out there when she must have gone," Jadwin said. He touched his notebook. "Your testimony. No one went down to the pool until Mr. Quist and Miss Morton went down at a quarter to two."

"It was a lovely night," David Lewis said. "She may just have decided to walk around her own garden in the moonlight. She was waiting for Mark to finish his work. Didn't feel like sleeping till Mark joined her. Unfortunately there was a killer on the loose."

"Not an illogical idea," Jadwin said. He closed his notebook. He opened the drawer of the carved Florentine desk beside which he was standing. He took out several sheets of notepaper and laid them on the top. "I don't see any particular reason for us to keep any of you here who don't live here," he said. "Unless, of course, there is some new, unexpected angle to the case. If you will just write down your names, addresses, and telephone numbers on these sheets of paper, you are free to go in the morning—or now, if you choose."

"It's almost morning now," Beatrice said. She was looking at the French windows through which a reddish, hot light showed on the eastern horizon.

Lydia was tugging at Quist's sleeve. "Aren't you going to tell him about the boy's car? Someone's lied to him about there being gas in it?"

Quist's face was set in hard lines. "Not now," he said.

Very few native New Yorkers have seen the sun rise over the city. It was particularly beautiful that morning, colors reflecting against towers of glass, as Quist drove his Mercedes down the East Side Drive. Lydia was sitting beside him and Bobby Hilliard and Marilyn were in the back seat. It was not a gay drive. Quist explained his position about Tiptoe's jalopy and its gas content.

"Lewis called the top brass somewhere—State Police, maybe the very top in Albany. The Lewis-Stillwell financial intricacies mustn't be disturbed. They have a ready fall guy in that unhappy Tiptoe character. They'll discredit his alibi at the Boat Club. Just to make sure, they'll discredit his story about being out of gas. If Bobby hadn't checked, we'd never have known. So they impound the car, put a little gas in it, and Tiptoe is a dead duck. Case closed. Gold star for Jadwin, Sims and company."

"And if you confront them with Bobby's evidence?"

"He was mistaken," Quist said. "He checked in a hurry and he somehow was mistaken."

"But he wasn't. So Tiptoe is innocent. So who—"

"The $64,000 question," Quist said, frowning.

"What are you going to do?"

"Check out on Brother Jadwin. Instinctively I trusted him. Maybe my radar system is out of order."

Quist dropped his passengers outside Lydia's apartment, which was only a couple of blocks from his Beekman Place establishment. Bobby and Marilyn went their separate ways in cabs. Then Quist garaged his car.

In his duplex apartment he got the percolator going in his kitchen, went upstairs for a shave, a shower, and a change of clothes. He looked as fresh as if he'd had a good eight hours' sleep instead of none when he came back downstairs. He poured himself coffee and went to the phone. A moment later he was talking to Lieutenant

Kreevich of New York's Homicide Division.

"Don't tell me you've dug up another corpse for me," Kreevich said.

"Not in your jurisdiction, pal," Quist said. "You know a detective in the State Police—Westchester—named Jadwin?"

"Well. He's a highly professional, good cop."

"Uncorruptible?"

"Meaning?"

"Could heat be brought on him from high up to falsify evidence?"

"In a murder case?"

"Yes."

"Never," Kreevich said flatly. "Things happen in this business, Quist. Go easy on this one, go easy on that one. Don't give the press a chance to smear this one or that one. Sometimes we listen. But fake evidence to convict the wrong man? Not me, not Jadwin."

Quist laid it out for the Lieutenant. "Lewis has pull, all the way to the White House," he concluded. "That car had no gas in it, but Jadwin says it did. At least he says Sims told him it did."

"He'd have no reason not to believe Sims," Kreevich said.

"Unless he's in on the coverup," Quist said. "Because someone is being covered, Lieutenant. The Tiptoe kid never did it."

"Did you tell Jadwin what you know?"

"I had to be sure I could trust him first," Quist said.

"Trust him," Kreevich said. "Steve Jadwin is clean as a whistle."

"Thanks."

"A hint, if you care," Kreevich said.

"I care."

"Who did David Lewis call on the phone? If it was an out-of-the-area call, it will be on Stillwell's phone bill. It might help to find out who got to Sims."

"Thanks again."

"Any time," Kreevich said.

Quist carried his coffee cup out into the terrace which overlooked the East River. The city was beginning to steam with the August heat. Frowning, he watched a tug pulling a bargeload of scrap iron down toward the harbor. Before too long, he thought, the world would be buried under junk, the rivers and oceans filled with it. Everything was being polluted in our society, including the truth. It was, he thought ironically, his business to help with that pollution. It was the public relations man's job to make people look better than they were, products more attractive than they were, even charities and causes more essential than they were. His job for Marilyn Martin was about as honest as they came. She made the clothes and he was to have gotten them seen. The potential customer had a free choice. But the designs would never be seen on Caroline. The coffee tasted bitter. God, what a thing to happen to her! Her life snuffed out, her loveliness defaced.

A muscle rippled along the line of Quist's jaw. The polluters were at work here, too—polluters of beauty, and truth, and justice. David Lewis's craggy face with its thick black brows floated before him. "I was calling the top brass in the State Police. They'll be sending someone from their detective division. I want a good, discreet man. If this is bungled, the media will turn it into a Roman holiday." What kind of a Roman holiday? Some scandal revealed? Personal guilt exposed? A business deal with Mark Stillwell that wouldn't bear the light of day? Never mind about Caroline; never mind a long-haired, hippie singer. Let two people die, but let's not have a Roman holiday.

Well, Caroline was not going to die without the right person paying for what had been done to her.

What in God's name could have taken Caroline down to the pool? Lydia's guess was sound. She hadn't been planning to swim. She must have started to undress. The beautiful gown she'd worn for the evening had been removed. She hadn't gotten to taking off her black lace underthings. Something had made her slip into a robe and slippers and go down to the pool. Something she saw? Someone had asked her to meet him, or her, there? In that case, her change of clothes would have been more suitable. She had, he thought, gone quickly, unexpectedly.

The telephone rang.

Quist put his coffee cup down on the parapet and went in to answer it.

"Mr. Quist?"

"Yes."

"Captain Jadwin here. I hope you weren't sleeping." The detective's voice sounded relaxed.

"Just going to the office," Quist said, wondering.

"I'm just starting into the city," Jadwin said. "Checking out on the Tiptoe boy. It seems he lives in the East Village."

"Oh."

"I have a feeling about you, Mr. Quist. At the end of our little session at the Stillwell house this morning I heard Miss Morton say to you, 'Aren't you going to tell him—' I lost the rest of it. It seems like a loose end. I hate loose ends. Is there something you didn't tell me?"

Quist hesitated. "Yes," he said.

"I'd like to come to see you. I should be in town in about an hour."

"I'll be in my office," Quist said, and gave him the address of the glass finger atop Grand Central Station.

"Coming here is a little like walking onto a movie set," Captain Jadwin said. He seemed not quite able to take his eyes off Connie Parmalee's long slim legs. She had guided him down the corridor to Quist's office from the reception room. He must have had an eyeful of the glamorous Miss Chard out there, Quist thought. "The colors, the modern paintings, the—the—"

"The dolls," Quist said, smiling.

"Comparing this to a State Police barracks, I have suddenly decided I'm in the wrong line of work," Jadwin said.

"This is what I call the 'image business,' " Quist said. "Our image is to be very modern, guiding the way to an exciting future." He turned to Connie. "If Bobby has come in, ask him to join us, love. And no calls till I tell you."

Jadwin, somewhat gingerly, took the chair Quist suggested and then looked surprised that anything made of aluminum tubes could be so comfortable. "Someday I would like the guided tour of this place," he said. "But time is a factor, Mr. Quist. Are you going to tell me what Miss Morton thought you should?"

"I checked out on you with Kreevich," Quist said. "I'd have called you if you hadn't called me."

Jadwin's gray eyes were lazily interested. He said nothing.

"Caroline Stillwell was an old friend, a client, going back to her days as an actress in films," Quist said. "I was very fond of her. More than anything else, at the moment, I want the person who killed her punished."

"That makes two of us," Jadwin said. "Fortunately we've got the killer."

"I don't think so."

"Oh? Playing detective again, Mr. Quist?"

"Yes, if you want to put it that way."

"Skip it," Jadwin said. "I'm listening."

"One thing I know for certain, Captain, is that Caroline was killed before Lydia and I went down to the pool. If it was Tiptoe who killed her, he had better than forty-five minutes in which to get away. Finding him on the grounds seemed providential for Sims, but I tended to believe his story. He said he hadn't left the Boat Club till two, that he ran out of gas in front of the Stillwell place and came in, looking for help. While he was nosing around the police car came. He hid, and before he could make a break for it, the second car came and he was caught."

"For the moment his Boat Club alibi holds up—but his friends would lie for him," Jadwin said. "But the 'out of gas' story simply isn't true. There was gas in his car. Plenty of gas."

The door to the office opened and Bobby Hilliard came in. He gave Jadwin his boyish, Jimmy Stewart smile.

"Hello, Mr. Hilliard."

"Hi," Bobby said.

"That's why I checked on you with Kreevich," Quist said. "There was no gas in that jalopy when we were all sent up to the house from the pool by Sims."

Jadwin's eyes stopped blinking.

"I didn't want Sims chasing off after the wrong person. I asked Bobby here to check the jalopy when we got up to the house."

"And?" Jadwin asked.

"It was bone-dry, Captain," Bobby said. "I took the cap off the tank and put a stick in it. Nothing. It wasn't even damp at the end."

Jadwin sat very still, very silent.

"In the house," Quist said, "David Lewis was making a phone call. He explained he'd been talking to the top brass in the State Police to make sure they sent a good man from the detective division. He wanted to be sure there was no Roman holiday. When you came and told us there was gas in the jalopy, I didn't trust you. Because that tank was empty, Captain, before Sims had it towed away."

There was a tense silence before Jadwin spoke. "You couldn't be mistaken, Mr. Hilliard? Your stick wasn't too short?"

"I broke it off a shrub," Bobby said. "It stuck a couple of feet out of the top of the tank. It hit solidly against the bottom of the tank. I worked it around down there. The tank was empty."

"I think you can understand why I hesitated talking to you," Quist said. "David Isham Lewis is a powerful man; if he was powerful enough to buy off the State Police, I was going to have to go it alone. Because I don't intend to have Caroline's murder brushed under the rug, Captain."

Jadwin drew a deep breath. He took a cigarette out of his pocket, put it in his mouth, but didn't light it. "I knocked off these things about six months ago," he said. "I still play with them, even if I don't smoke them." He was stalling for time, thinking. "Let me tell you something, Quist. There's always a rotten apple in every barrel. A rotten cop—I suppose even someone rotten in your business. I've known Sims for twenty years. Not very imaginative; pretty much of a 'by the book' kind of man. But honest! I swear to that. He told me there was gas in the tank, I believe it."

"And not us?" Quist asked in a flat voice.

"Of course I believe you," Jadwin said. "When Mr. Hilliard checked it, the gas tank was empty. When Sims checked it—or had it checked—there was gas in it. Those two things can both be true."

"Then who did Lewis get to?"

"Maybe no one, in the sense you mean," Jadwin said. "I mean no one on the Trooper force. Maybe he did talk to someone at the top. Big shots like Lewis always think they can impress less important people. But I can tell you that my being put on the case was routine. I was on duty, I wasn't working on anything else, I was at the top of the list. I wasn't chosen as a suppressor of Roman holidays. It was my turn."

"But Lewis got to someone."

"Let's stay factual, Quist. All we have is that the gas tank was empty when Mr. Hilliard checked it, and later it had gas in it. Tying Lewis's phone call into it is guesswork. You think the gas was put into the tank after the car was towed away, which implicated troopers. Right?"

"It seems likely."

"There are four cars and several power mowers and tractors in Stillwell's garage back of the house," Jadwin said. "They have their own gas pump. It would have been no problem for someone on the grounds—a member of the household, servants, chauffeur, gardener—to put some gas in a can and take it down to Tiptoe's jalopy. Mr. Hilliard was able to go to it without attracting attention. Someone else could have got to it later. In my book of probabilities, Quist, if Lewis got to someone, it was someone in the household. You see, I trust cops."

"But you think, as I do, that Tiptoe is innocent?"

"I think it's entirely possible."

"So does he have to stay in jail?"

"I think so—for a while," Jadwin said. "If we're right about him, then he will do us the most good locked up. The minute he's freed, it will be obvious we're looking somewhere else. Right now the person we want thinks we think we've solved the case. Let's keep his guard down." Jadwin stood up. "Interesting morning. I'll want an official statement from you, Mr. Hilliard."

"Of course."

"Kreevich suggested we try to trace that call Lewis made. If it was out of the area, it would show up on Stillwell's bill," Quist said.

"If we can dig it out of some goddamned computer somewhere," Jadwin said. "Thanks for your help. Would I sound cold-blooded if I said you'd made the ball game a lot more interesting than I thought it was?"

The day developed into what most days were like in the offices of Julian Quist Associates. Clients and would-be clients stormed the place, all of them wanting to see Quist, most of them being sidetracked to one of his assistants and, in the long run, being quite happy about it.

It was a good day, a profitable day from a business point of view. Daniel Garvey, Quist's right-hand man in the business, came in with a big account that he'd been gunning for some time. It was a contract to promote a huge Sports Complex to be built outside the city—a domed, all-weather stadium to seat 80,000 people, ice rink and basketball arena, tennis courts, squash courts, swimming pools, and a race track to accommodate both thoroughbreds and trotters. It was going to take about four years to build.

"And we will be paid to keep it in the public eye every day of those four years," Garvey told Quist.

Dan Garvey was the complete physical opposite of Quist —dark, brooding, conservative as to clothes. They were both a little over six feet tall, but Garvey weighed a good twenty pounds more, not an ounce of it fat. He had been a promising professional football player when a knee injury cut his career short. He was good-looking enough to have had a career in films if he hadn't gone to work for Julian Quist Associates. He was just the right man to have in your corner if the action got physical. Hidden away in his private treasures was a Phi Beta Kappa key, which he had never mentioned to anyone.

"You had a rough night," Garvey said.

"Rough," Quist said. He drew a sharp picture of Caroline's murder, and an account of his recent interview with Jadwin. "There is still a killer on the loose, and we haven't even got a smell of him."

Garvey was frowning. "Coincidence, of course," he said. "The contracts for our job on this Sports Complex are in the legal department at the moment, already signed by the president of the company that's financing it—David Isham Lewis."

"He's financing it?"

"If you cut away the corporate embroidery. Two hundred million bucks is the estimate. All out of one pocket. You think he may have bribed somebody to put gas in that jalopy?"

"Somebody did. No evidence that it was Lewis."

"Every once in a while I get sick at my stomach when I cross the path of one of these super-rich guys," Garvey said. "You realize if he wanted someone to put five gallons of gas in that car he could pay them enough to retire for life and not feel it? That's power, dad."

"Does he stand to make money out of this Sports Complex?"

"Money? It hurts to think about it. Rentals to major league baseball teams, football teams, the works. Concessions. Parking. And on and on. A cut of this, a piece of that. He'll double what he's put into it in five years."

"We've in the wrong business," Quist said.

"I like it," Garvey said. "It's nice to know that what you're involved in is clean. Nobody bottom-dealing."

Connie Parmalee, Quist's secretary, appeared in the doorway.

"Lieutenant Kreevich is on the phone," she said. "I thought you'd talk to him."

"Sure," Quist said. He leaned forward and switched on the squawkbox on his desk, so that the call was audible to all three of them. "Yes, Lieutenant?"

Kreevich's voice sounded hard and cold. "Did Steve Jadwin come to see you this morning?"

"Left here about an hour ago. You are right about him."

"I *was* right," Kreevich said, with a peculiar emphasis on the verb. "I'd like to talk to you."

"Fine. Where are you?"

"Downstairs in the Station. Be with you in five minutes. Are you sitting down?"

"Yes."

"Jadwin was making a phone call in a pay booth down here. Must have been right after he left you. Someone pumped him full of lead."

Quist sat very still. "Is he badly hurt?"

Kreevich's voice exploded in anger. "He's dead, goddamn it!"

Part Two

chapter 1

Hundreds of people, milling around in Grand Central Station, were close enough to see what happened to Captain Jadwin, but nobody really did. There was a long row of phone booths just outside an entrance to the Commodore Hotel. People came in and out of the revolving door there; scores more poured in from the Lexington Avenue entrance and to and from the subway. The booths were usually filled, with people waiting.

There had been shots. Five or six shots, people said. They had heard, but they had not seen the gunman. What they saw was Jadwin, vomiting blood, clutching at his bloodstained shirt, stagger out of the booth and fall. Nobody remembered seeing anyone run away. The best guess was that the killer had emptied his gun at Jadwin, probably standing right in the door of the booth, and then mingled, calmly, with the people who crowded in. He had eventually left, unhurried, unsuspected, with no attempt made to stop him because no one had pointed a finger at him.

A railroad cop was one of the first people on the scene. His primary job was to keep people from trampling on the dead man. People always come forward with excited accounts of what they've seen and heard, but there was no clear identification. One had seen a suspicious-looking fat man hurrying off toward the information booth. Another had seen a woman who had dashed through the revolving door into the Commodore. A reasonably calm businessman, standing in line at the next booth only a few feet away, hadn't, in all the general station noise, been certain where the shots had come from until Jadwin almost stumbled into him.

"The sonofabitch disappeared like the Invisible Man," Lieutenant Kreevich said. He was a short, square man with a boyish face that was flushed with anger. "Nobody saw a damn thing that adds up."

Quist and Garvey had listened to Kreevich's story, Quist shocked by the bloody picture the detective had drawn. It could have nothing to do with the Stillwell case, he told himself, and didn't believe a word of it.

"How did you make your appointment with Jadwin?" Kreevich asked.

"He called me on the phone and said he wanted to see me. He'd heard Lydia ask me if I wasn't going to tell him —something. It was about the empty gas tank, but I hadn't told him at the time because I wanted to check out on him with you before I did."

"Where did he call from?"

"I don't know. He said he was coming into town to do some checking on the Tiptoe boy. I assumed he was calling from the country, either the police barracks or the Stillwell place. It takes a little less than an hour to drive in. He was here about an hour and a quarter after he made the call."

"If someone heard him talking to you—" Kreevich said. "What did he say to you?"

Quist tried to remember exactly. "He said he'd heard Lydia ask me if I wasn't going to tell him—something. Would I tell him; it seemed like a loose end and he hated loose ends. Was there something I hadn't told him?"

"If somebody heard that they'd know you had something that might turn his attention away from Tiptoe," Kreevich said. "If they were going to play rough, why didn't they try to shut you up before you could tell whatever it was you knew?"

Quist shrugged. "When I told Jadwin what I knew, he saw his case falling apart. Either someone on the State Police or someone in the house had filled that jalopy with gas so the case would be tight against Tiptoe. He trusted the police. He said they'd keep Tiptoe in jail for a while so no one would guess they were looking somewhere else. That was it.

"It shouldn't be too hard to find out who left the place in Westchester, cop or civilian, about the same time that Jadwin left," Quist suggested. "He must have started in as soon as he got through talking to me. No chance to get to me ahead of him unless they'd wrecked him on the way in."

Dan Garvey turned away from the window where he'd been standing, hands jammed deep in his pockets. "You're dealing with power on a big scale out there," he said. "I'm talking about David Lewis and Mark Stillwell. It sounds melodramatic, but neither one of them had to follow Jadwin to stop him or to silence you, Julian. They pick up the phone, call a connection here in town, and a paid killer puts on his hat and heads for where the action is."

Kreevich lit a cigarette and took a deep drag on it. "The record on Mark Stillwell's phone could make interesting reading," he said. "Who did Lewis call last night when he said he'd been talking to the top brass in the State Police? Did Jadwin call you from there, Quist? After that, did someone make a call to the city for a man with a gun?" He picked up Quist's phone and called headquarters. He asked for a record of all out-of-the-area calls made on Mark Stillwell's phone in the last twelve hours. My position is an interesting one," he said, when he'd hung up. "I have no jurisdiction out there in the country, but Jadwin was working on the Stillwell case and Jadwin is my baby. The State police have to cooperate with me, and the Stillwell gang are part of my ball game whether they like it or not. I want you to go out there with me, Quist."

"Why?"

"You touch both cases. You know the people out there and you can help me. Most important, if you're seen with me, someone will know it's too late to try to keep you from talking."

"You seriously think I might be a target?" Quist asked.

"I'll feel better when they know it won't do them any good," Kreevich said.

Quist picked up the phone and asked if Lydia had come into the office yet. She hadn't. He hesitated as he started to dial her number. She needed sleep after last night.

"Will you tell Lydia where I've gone and why, when she comes in?" he asked Garvey.

Garvey nodded. "Stay close to Kreevich till they know you've done your talking, chum," he said. "Mind if I do a little checking on our new client, Mr. Lewis? It will seem normal enough since we're going to be promoting his

Sports Complex. Maybe I can get a lead to where he goes when he wants to buy muscle."

"Play it cool," Kreevich said. "I don't want anyone running for cover before I'm ready."

When Kreevich got through with them, the State Police in the Parkhurst Barracks were in a state of shock. The commanding officer, a gray-haired veteran named Miller with the rank of Captain, Lieutenant Sims, and Sergeant Pollet took the news of Jadwin's murder hard. And as Kreevich put it to them, their own integrity was in question. Someone had put gas in Tiptoe's jalopy. Kreevich suggested it could have been a trooper, handsomely bribed or acting under orders from someone above him in the chain of command.

They protested, of course.

"We didn't examine that jalopy in any detail until after we'd been there for quite a while," Lieutenant Sims said. "There was so much else to do, so many people to handle. When I first arrived with a trooper named Worthing, we saw the jalopy. We stopped and Worthing looked in the glove compartment for a license or registration. Nothing. Then we caught sight of Tiptoe hiding in the shrubbery and we grabbed him. We didn't have his story till a little later. There was plenty of time to check out the gas tank. It didn't seem important to us."

"Oh?" Kreevich's baby face was rock-hard.

"There didn't seem any doubt to us that he was our man, whether his story stood up or not."

"When did you actually check the tank?"

"When Captain Jadwin arrived, I told him I wanted to have the jalopy towed into the lot where we take impounded cars. There was light there to go over it in detail —for fingerprints or any other evidence. He agreed. We had it towed in. That was almost an hour after we first arrived. When it was at the lot, our men went over it and found the tank was half-full, so we thought we knew Tiptoe had lied to us."

"So somebody put gas in it sometime after you arrived," Kreevich said.

"If you buy Mr. Quist's story," Miller said, giving Quist an unfriendly look.

"I buy it," Kreevich said. "I'm not accusing your men, you understand, Captain. There's a gas pump on the Stillwell property. They have cars, maintenance machinery for the grounds. Someone connected with the Stillwell household could have done it."

The phone rang on Miller's desk and he answered it. "For you," he said to Kreevich.

Kreevich spoke to someone he obviously knew, took a piece of paper from Miller's desk, and wrote on it as he listened. Finally he thanked the caller and put down the phone. He stared for a moment at the sheet of paper.

"There were six out-of-area calls made on the Stillwell phone since midnight," he said. "Three of them to the same number. It's the phone of a big-shot lawyer in New York named Max Gottfried. One of his clients is David Lewis. Another call went to a Dr. Frankel, also in the city. Dr. Frankel is a psychoanalyst. The third call went to the offices of Marilyn Martin." Kreevich looked at Quist. "Finally a call to your office, which must have been Jadwin."

"Marilyn was designing a whole line of clothes for Mrs. Stillwell," Quist said. "She probably called her people to tell them to stop work on it. Caroline wasn't going to need the dresses that were in the works."

"Lewis said he was calling the 'top brass' in the State Police," Kreevich said. "No number here to indicate such a call."

"If he had called here," Miller said, "which he didn't, it wouldn't show. Local call. If he'd called someone higher up —in Albany or somewhere else—it would show."

"But it doesn't," Kreevich said. He folded the piece of paper and put it in his pocket. "I'm going out to the Stillwell place, Captain. I'm going to be crossing your path, getting in your way if you don't choose to work with me. I think we're after the same person or persons, because Tiptoe doesn't make sense. Do we work together or not?"

"Together," Miller said. "Glad of your help. We want this cop-killing sonofabitch just as badly as you do. Jadwin was an old friend of mine. We were in the same group of trainees twenty-odd years ago." He turned to Sims. "It's your case, Lieutenant. You satisfied?"

"Jadwin backed you up a hundred percent when I saw him, Lieutenant," Quist said.

"Glad to go along," Sims said.

"It will be interesting to know who needed a psychiatrist in the early hours of a Saturday morning," Kreevich said.

On that hot, hazy August day the Stillwell place looked magnificent, set back from the main highway on a rise of ground, with its perfectly manicured lawns and gardens.

"We're probably not going to find Lewis here," Quist said to Kreevich as they drove up the winding, bluestone drive. "Jadwin gave us all permission to leave. But someone heard Jadwin call me."

He was wrong about Lewis. He was almost the first person they saw, sitting on a side terrace with Beatrice Lorimer. There were coffee cups and the remains of a brunch on the table between them. Mrs. Lorimer's elegant eyebrows went up as she saw Quist.

"Julian, you've come back!" It was the first time she'd used his first name.

"For an unfortunate reason," Quist said. He was watching Lewis. The tycoon's craggy face was bland, apparently not too interested. "This is Lieutenant Kreevich of Manhattan's Homicide Squad."

"Something new on Tiptoe?" Lewis asked. He picked up his coffee cup and sipped.

"Captain Jadwin, who was in charge of the case here, was shot to death in Grand Central Station a couple of hours ago," Kreevich said.

"Oh, my God!" Mrs. Lorimer said, her hands gripping the arms of her wicker chair.

Lewis put down his coffee cup. "I suppose most policemen have enemies," he said.

"Jadwin made a call from here to Quist in New York," Kreevich said. "He knew Quist was withholding evidence. He discussed it with Quist on the phone, and told him he was on his way to New York. We think someone may have overheard him, determined to stop him before or after the fact. It was after the fact. Quist had told him what he knew. He has also told me."

"Withholding evidence is rather serious, isn't it, Quist?" Lewis asked.

"Mr. Quist's reason for holding back seems justified to me," Kreevich said. "The police told you all that they'd found gas in Tiptoe's car, which seemed to prove Tiptoe had been lying. But Quist's friend, Mr. Hilliard, had checked the car and found the gas tank empty. Either the police or someone else had put gas in the car after Mr. Hilliard checked it. Quist wasn't sure who he could tell what he knew. He checked out with me when he got back to town—checked on Jadwin, who was, I told him, to be trusted. So he agreed to tell Jadwin."

"You think one of us—someone in this household—filled the tank?" Mrs. Lorimer asked, her knuckles showing white from the tightness of her grip on the chair arms.

Lewis smiled, a faintly ironic smile. "Of course the police couldn't have done it—to shore up their case against Tiptoe?"

"We thought of that," Kreevich said. "You had told Quist you had just called the top brass in the State Police to make sure a discreet detective took over the investigation of Mrs. Stillwell's murder. To prevent a 'Roman holiday,' you said. But you didn't make such a call, Mr. Lewis. We've checked the out-of-area calls."

Lewis's dark eyebrows drew together, and his smile faded. "Figure of speech," he said. "Actually I called my lawyer in New York and asked him to get onto the 'top brass.' "

"Max Gottfried?"

"You do your homework, Lieutenant," Lewis said. He smiled again, a small quirk at the corner of his straight mouth. "I like a man who knows the answers to questions before he asks them. Keeps him working on solid ground."

"You called Gottfried twice more after that," Kreevich said.

"Yes, I did. I mean, you have the record, you say."

"Care to tell me why?"

The smile disappeared. "I don't think I'm required to answer your questions, Lieutenant."

"You're not at the moment. But is there any reason why you shouldn't?"

Lewis actually laughed. "Adroit, Lieutenant; very adroit. No real reason, except I don't like to be pushed. You weren't here early this morning. You didn't know Mrs. Stillwell. Perhaps you can guess, though, that we were all in a state of shock. How much do you know about me?"

"What everyone else knows," Kreevich said. "Financial colossus."

"If you know anything about the world of finance, Lieutenant, you'll know that it's a world of many intricate patterns and maneuvers. A little thing, out of balance, can destroy a mountain of work."

"A little thing like a murder?" Quist asked.

Lewis looked at him with something like contempt. "Yes, a little thing like a murder," he said. "Caroline Stillwell was a beautiful and charming woman. I was shocked by what happened to her, grieved for Mark. But I was also concerned about my mountain, gentlemen. Being connected, even remotely, with a murder might bring part of that mountain tumbling down around our ears. I couldn't leave here, or handle things from here. So I put it in the hands of a trusted associate—my lawyer. I called him as I had thoughts about the matter."

"And you also called a Dr. Frankel?"

Lewis's face went blank. "Who is Dr. Frankel?"

"That is my next question," Kreevich said. He turned to Beatrice Lorimer.

"I don't know any Dr. Frankel," she said.

"He is a psychiatrist—an analyst."

"Rings no bells," Lewis said.

Kreevich glanced at his notebook. "Did either of you hear Jadwin making a telephone call to Mr. Quist this morning?"

Lewis shook his head slowly, as if he was trying to remember.

"We had turned over the library to Captain Jadwin and the State Police," Beatrice Lorimer said. "He must have made the call from there, which was, in a sense, private."

"But there are extension phones over which a call could have been heard," Kreevich said.

"There are at least half a dozen," Beatrice said. "There is also an entirely separate system—different numbers—connected with Mark's study. An unlisted number."

Kreevich frowned. He'd missed something. There was a second phone line to check on. "Can you give me a list of the servants, Mrs. Lorimer—those in the house, chauffeurs, gardeners, anyone else?"

"Of course."

"If you would, please. And now I'd like to see Mr. Mark Stillwell, Mr. Jerry Stillwell, Mr. Patrick Grant, and Mrs. Lewis." He ticked the names off in his book.

"I'm sorry, but Mark and Pat Grant have gone down to the mortuary—to make arrangements," Beatrice said. "You'll probably find Jerry in his studio at the bottom of the garden." She gestured.

"I'm afraid Mrs. Lewis can't talk to anyone," Lewis said. "She went into a state of hysterical shock when Caroline was found. We had to call in the local doctor. She's under sedation and there's a practical nurse with her."

"Local doctor?"

"Dr. Tabor," Beatrice said. "We hardly know him. Nobody in this household ever gets sick." She tried a laugh, and it sounded brittle.

"My wife's condition is why I am still here," Lewis said, "instead of in my office, where I should be."

"If you would make that list of the servants for me, Mrs. Lorimer," Kreevich said. "I'd particularly like to talk to the chauffeur and the head gardener at the moment."

The garage on the Stillwell place, located back of the house, would have seemed like luxury living to some people. There was space for five cars, plus a shop space equipped with endless tools and a lift so that the Stillwell automobiles could be serviced on the spot. On the second floor was a luxurious apartment in which Lukins, the chauffeur, lived. The first thing Quist noticed was a gasoline pump, located just outside the doors to the building.

They found Lukins, wearing a rubber apron, washing down a sleek-looking Porsche. He was a muscular, dark young man, handsome and voluble. He liked to talk—to gossip, Quist suspected—without hesitation. He didn't appear to be a man with anything to hide. He didn't seem to be shocked by the two murders.

"Violence is a bad scene," he said, "but it's like every day in this man's world. You wait for it to happen to you when you walk down the street at night."

He had been with the Stillwells for five years. Great people to work for. His job—to keep five cars in shape, mostly drive Mrs. Lorimer and Caroline places. Mark and Patrick Grant liked to drive their own cars. This Porsche was Grant's. Mark drove a Corvette convertible. He and Grant had used it to go into town. Yes, he serviced the cars, kept them gassed up.

"Last night," Kreevich said. It was a question.

"You could call it a night off for me," Lukins said. "Party. I wouldn't be needed. I—uh—had a guest. A doll. I wasn't sleeping, if you see what I mean." He smiled a bright, very white smile. "Like Mr. Quist here, I wasn't sleeping. Sorry to sound like a peeping Tom, Mr. Quist, but we saw you come down to the pool with your lady friend —saw you take off your robes. Wow!"

"Where did you see them from?" Kreevich asked.

Lukins gestured upward. "There's a window seat inside those casement windows up there. My doll and I were sitting there, having a drink and looking at the moonlight. We saw Mr. Quist and his lady come down from the house. Like I said, wow!"

"How long had you been sitting there?"

"Not long. I don't like to kiss and tell," Lukins said, his smile suggesting that he loved it. "We'd had a few drinks earlier, and I hustled my doll for a while and then she—very obligingly—gave in. We had quite an evening. We were in what you might call an intermission when I thought I heard someone snooping around outside."

"When was that?"

"About twenty past one o'clock. I know, because the doll had just looked at my wall clock and said she ought to be going home. I was trying to convince her it was just the shank of the evening." He hesitated. "Another way to nail down the time was that I'd just heard Tommy Bayne—Mr. Bayne—leave the big house in his car."

"So you heard something. What kind of something?"

"Rustling around in the bushes outside. Could have been someone, I thought, looking to steal something out of the garage here. There's plenty of valuable stuff to steal. It could have been somebody trying to make out with some chick. Anyway, I got off the bed and went to the window to have a look. Presently my doll joined me. We couldn't see anyone or anything, and we didn't hear anything more. I suggested a drink, and we sat on the window seat and had a couple. That's when we saw Mr. Quist and his lady come down from the house."

"Did it occur to you that you might have heard someone butchering Mrs. Stillwell?" Kreevich asked.

"Jesus, no! I mean we didn't know anything like that had happened. We were back in bed when we heard the siren. My doll grabbed up her clothes and split. Her car was down by the service entrance. I don't think anybody saw her."

"I'd like to see her to confirm your story," Kreevich said.

"Oh, come off it, Lieutenant. Do you have to drag her into it? I mean—well, she's got a husband! She can't tell you any more than I've told you."

"We'll see," Kreevich said. "What did you do after she left?"

"Got dressed—and waited for somebody to call me."

"You didn't go down to the pool where the action was?"

"Stay away from cops till they ask to see you is my motto."

"So you stayed here for the next couple of hours?"

"When I was dressed, I came down from my apartment and stood right outside there in the open. I wasn't hiding if anybody wanted me."

"If you were standing out here, you must have had that gas pump in sight."

"Sure."

"Who pumped some gas out of it?"

Lukins looked surprised. "Nobody. Nobody pumped any

74

gas out of it any time last night. I'd have heard it."

"Even when you were being—active upstairs?"

"It's got an electric motor," Lukins said. "Each time you pump a gallon a little bell rings. Just like in a filling station."

"Where else could anyone get gas on the grounds here?"

"Maybe in the gardener's tool shop. He keeps the lawn mowers and a couple of garden tractors there. He usually fills the tractors from the pump here, but he has a couple of ten-gallon cans that he fills and takes down to the tool shop for the mowers." Lukins turned his head. "Here comes the boss, back from town."

The gray Corvette pulled to a stop outside the garage. Patrick Grant was driving it. Mark Stillwell, slumped in the passenger's seat, seemed not to realize they had arrived until Grant touched his arm. Both men were wearing dark glasses.

Mark seemed to have trouble pulling himself out of the car. He look bone-weary.

"Julian! You're back," he said. His voice was hoarse with fatigue.

Quist introduced Kreevich and told them about Jadwin. As he talked, Mark put both hands on the front fender of the Corvette and leaned forward, as though he was going to be sick.

"This is too much," he said. "Too much!"

Grant had listened, a little tense, but not tired. "I'd better get back up to the house," he said. "Does Lewis know?"

"He knows."

"It's a damn bad time for all this notoriety," Grant said. "There are phone calls to be made, Mark." He turned to go.

"Just a minute, Mr. Grant," Kreevich said. "Did you or Mr. Stillwell hear Jadwin making a call to Mr. Quist early this morning?"

Grant shook his head. "Mark and I were in his study. The phones there are on different lines from the house phones."

Kreevich looked suddenly angry. "Business as usual?" he asked. "An autopsy being done on Mrs. Stillwell and business as usual?"

"You sonofabitch," Mark said, still leaning against the car.

"What would you do if your wife had been brutally murdered, Kreevich?" Grant asked. A nerve twitched on his bronzed cheek. "You'd do anything you could to keep from going crazy! You've got a hell of a nerve suggesting that Mark wasn't sick with grief."

"Let it go, Pat," Mark said, his voice gone dull. He lifted the dark glasses to Kreevich. "Sorry I lost my temper, old boy. I'm not quite myself, as you may guess. Does this thing about the gas tank mean you don't think Tiptoe is our man after all?"

"Almost certainly not," Kreevich said.

Mark bent down over the car again, and Patrick Grant seemed to have frozen in his tracks.

"Technically, there are two investigations in progress, Mr. Stillwell," Kreevich said. "The State Police are charged with bringing your wife's killer in. I am after the man—or woman—who shot Captain Jadwin. But the two cases are so closely interlocked that, you might say, they become one. That's why Lieutenant Sims isn't here now—or anyone else from the State Police. They've left this to me while they get Tiptoe cleaned up and swept away."

"I find myself pretty goddam annoyed with all this police double talk," Grant said. The sun reflected in two bright little spots on his black glasses. "Gas tank, gas tank, who filled the gas tank? Tiptoe was here, where he shouldn't have been. He had a knife. I haven't heard anything about the lab report on that knife. His alibi as to time can't be taken too seriously. Now, for some reason, you choose to have him swept under the rug. Your phrase, not mine, Lieutenant. You said 'swept away.' "

"So we can get at the truth," Kreevich said.

"So you involve Mark, and David Lewis, and the rest of us. You'll be sure to get your name in the paper that way!"

"Easy, Pat," Mark said, not looking up.

"Why us?" Grant shouted, very angry now. "If it wasn't Tiptoe, then it could have been some other tramp, some other passing thief, out to find himself some drug money! Someone you haven't even dreamed of so far. Why us? We loved Caroline! All of us loved her, god damn it! Oh, maybe not the Lewises. They'd only just met her, but for that reason they had no motive to hate her, to kill her. Let us decently mourn the passing of someone we all loved, and go after the real killer. He's probably miles away, not even in this state by now!"

"Two questions, Mr. Grant," Kreevich said, unruffled. "Why did someone fill the gas tank in Tiptoe's car sometime after the murder had been discovered and after the troopers were already here?"

"How the hell do I know?" Grant said, still in a high key. "Maybe some trooper wanted to move the car, put gas in it, and when he found it was a blunder, decided to keep his mouth shut. Maybe some other creeps from the Boat Club thought they could help Tiptoe by moving his car, but lost their nerve after they'd got gas in it. Maybe the real murderer wanted to use it to get away in, but was too late, or couldn't get it started. Why must it have been someone trying to pin a bum rap on Tiptoe?"

"You'd make a good lawyer for the defendant—when we have one," Kreevich said.

"And why does Jadwin's murder have to be connected with the situation here?" Grant said. "He's been a policeman for years. He's sent a hell of a lot of people to jail, who hated him for it. Someone, unconnected with us, saw him in that phone booth, blew his stack, and shot him then and there. Unrelated—totally unrelated to Caroline or the case Jadwin was working on. Coincidence! An unhappy coincidence."

"My second question," Kreevich said, as though he hadn't heard, "is why did Mrs. Stillwell come down to the pool area last night when she was in the process of getting ready for bed? If she saw a prowler, it doesn't seem she'd have tried to handle the situation without help. If she'd thought of swimming, she'd have been dressed for it. The way she was dressed suggests it was a spur-of-the-moment decision. Or perhaps she was in the habit of wandering around the grounds in the night—wearing bedroom slippers that would be ruined by the dew-soaked grass."

Mark raised his head. "I've been struggling to find the answer to that question for hours," he said. "Caroline was a person of great spirit and courage—but not physical courage. If she'd seen a prowler, she'd have called me, or Pat, or Shallert, our houseman, or Lukins in the garage. She'd never have gone out there alone to face possible physical danger."

"The bedroom slippers suggest she hadn't simply decided

to go out for a stroll around the grounds," Kreevich said. "They were badly stained by the wet grass. She'd have known they would be. Not dressed for swimming; not really dressed to go out at all. It suggests she saw something or someone that made her hurry out to the place where she was killed, without stopping to put on proper shoes or clothes."

"I wish I could explain it," Mark said. "If she saw someone hurt—or perhaps one of our pets. We have two small dogs—corgis, and there are several cats that have attached themselves to us. If one of them was in trouble, she might have hurried out to help."

It was a reasonable explanation, Quist thought. Most reasonable except the real one, which involved someone with a knife and a thirst for blood. Or was it possible she had, in fact, hurried out to help one of the pets and stumbled, quite by accident, on the killer. Waiting there for what?

Mark's shock and grief seemed real enough, but Quist found himself still suffering from a slow burn over some of the reactions: Lewis afraid for his "mountain," Beatrice concerned for herself and the other members of the household, Grant unwilling to cooperate, Lukins concerned only about his married girl friend. Caroline was forgotten. Caroline lying on a slab in the morgue, her body further mutilated by the autopsy surgeon. Quist found himself suspecting each and every one of them; suspecting the power of money to protect a killer. Jadwin's death a coincidence? That he didn't buy. Jadwin, a dedicated and an honest cop, was a threat to someone. He'd been stopped in his tracks before he'd been able to weave his case together.

"A painful question, Mr. Stillwell," Kreevich said. "Let's

suppose your wife did see one of your dogs, his collar, let's say, tangled in the shrubbery. She hurried down to free the animal and found herself face to face with a killer—a man armed with a knife. To keep your wife from screaming for help, he stabs her."

"Oh, God," Mark whispered.

"But he went further than that, Mr. Stillwell. He stabbed her—once, twice. But then he ripped away her robe, tore off the brassiere she was wearing, and proceeded with a methodical mutilation."

"Do you have to go through this?" Grant demanded.

"It brings us to one of two conclusions," Kreevich said. "Either the killer was a psychotic, a degenerate, or—"

"Of course he was a psychotic!" Grant said. "Another Charles Manson, a drug-driven monster."

"—or it was someone who hated Mrs. Stillwell so passionately that killing her wasn't enough. Is there such a person, Mr. Stillwell?"

"No! No, of course not!" Mark said, still bending over the car fender.

"Some man she had rejected?" Kreevich asked quietly. "Some woman who thought Mrs. Stillwell had stolen her man?"

"You bastard! I ought to take you apart!" Grant said, taking a step toward the detective.

"I urge you not to try, Mr. Grant," Kreevich said. "I'm sorry to ask this kind of question, Mr. Stillwell. I chose to do it here, with only your friends present, instead of at a formal interrogation. Men must have flocked around your wife. She was extraordinarily attractive. She came from a background, before your marriage, where promiscuity is not frowned on—the theater, films. Could it have been someone in that past?"

Very slowly Mark straightened up and faced the detective. "I can understand, Lieutenant, why someone who didn't know Caroline could ask that question. I also understand that you are doing your job. Caroline and I have been married for about six years. Our sixth anniversary was to have been celebrated next month. She had been in films for about ten years before we married. She was thirty then, and a star of sorts. She knew, and worked with, and socialized with all the top personalities in Hollywood. I concede it was a different world than mine. Would you believe it if I told you I never asked her any questions about that time before I met her?"

"I'll listen," Kreevich said.

"I met her in Acapulco. I was on the Coast on business and went to Mexico for a house party weekend with one of my business associates. Caroline was there, and I fell in love with her on sight. I proposed to her after two days and she—she accepted me, dropped her career, became totally mine." Mark's voice broke. "We were married in California a few days later. It—it was the most impulsive thing I'd ever done in my life. We were in love, wildly—but physically in love, Lieutenant. We actually had to get to know each other. There were unspoken rules. I never asked her about her life up to then—except gossip and anecdotes. No 'did you ever' questions. She never asked me about my past. We grew together and it was much more binding than I could have hoped. I am so damned involved with my business life. She never complained; went with me if I asked her to—to Europe, to South America, to the Far East. She stayed at home alone if I couldn't take her. I never even thought of not trusting her. She wouldn't go to parties without me, or give parties in any of our homes without me. There was never even the shadow of a doubt in my mind as to her loyalty. Men, as you suggest, flocked around her when we did go places together, but I was never jealous— only proud that she belonged to me."

It was a better speech, Quist thought, than he might have expected from Mark. Perhaps tragedy had diverted him from his own power ego. He made Caroline's devotion to him seem more understandable.

"To give you an example, Lieutenant," Mark went on, "of Caroline's loyalty to me. This party, this weekend, had a special reason for taking place. Julian Quist had approached Caroline with a proposition from one of his clients, Marilyn Martin, the clothes designer. Caroline was to be paid ten thousand dollars for wearing Miss Martin's gowns at a variety of public functions. Caroline refused at first because she knew I couldn't go to all the opening nights, parties, balls, that Miss Martin wanted her to attend. Caroline didn't want to go to these affairs unescorted, and she felt I wouldn't like her going with some other man. Julian approached me about it. I thought Caroline would enjoy the change in her social life; be glad of her own earned pocket money. I suggested my brother Jerry could take her places without starting any unpleasant gossip. It was arranged that way, but only when I agreed. Caroline wouldn't have it any other way."

"And did your brother take her places?" Kreevich asked.

"It hadn't started. This weekend was to be what Julian called 'a dry run.' There would be a few people in and out. The Lewises, by the way, were last-minute and unexpected additions to the weekend. Caroline would wear some of Miss Martin's clothes, and Miss Martin and Julian would listen to how women reacted to them. If Miss Martin was satisfied, Caroline would have begun appearing in public with Jerry as her escort when I couldn't make it."

Kreevich closed his notebook. "Thanks for being so direct with me, Mr. Stillwell."

Mark lifted his head. It seemed to require a genuine effort, his fatigue was so great. "Are you still toying with the idea that someone in our household may have—might have—" He couldn't go on.

"We haven't really broken from the starting gate yet, Mr. Stillwell," Kreevich said.

Quist and Kreevich found Jerry Stillwell in his studio at the far end of the grounds. Like the main house, the studio was built of weathered stone, covered by a lush growth of ivy. It must have been a guest cottage originally, consisting of several rooms, a kitchen, a couple of baths. Partitions had, however, been knocked out to create one very large studio room, with a huge window cut into the north side to provide proper light. This main room was cluttered with paintings, sculpture, lithographs, and the tools of the artist's trade. The casual glimpse Quist had of Jerry's work surprised him. He was good—damn good; his colors bold and bright, his techniques revealing an unexpected vitality. Jerry shouldn't have been hidden away, Quist thought, dependent on his brother for financial support. Properly handled, Jerry Stillwell should have been making it big on his own.

Jerry was stretched out in a deck chair on the terrace of his cottage, his face turned toward the sun, his eyes closed.

He seemed startled when Quist spoke to him.

"Julian! I thought you were long gone."

"Gone and come back," Quist said. "No one from the big house has talked to you since we got back?" He introduced Kreevich.

"No one pays much attention to me," Jerry said. "Now that Caroline's gone, no one will."

Quist told him why they were back, what had happened to Jadwin, the certainty that Johnny Tiptoe was innocent. While he talked, Jerry pulled himself slowly up out of the chair. His eyes had a dazed look. He fumbled in the pocket of his plaid sports shirt for a cigarette. Quist held his lighter for him.

"Bitch!" he said.

Quist's eyebrows rose.

"Beatrice," Jerry said. "Bitch! She wouldn't bother to let me know what was cooking."

"She probably thought Mark would tell you."

"Not Beatrice. She'd know damn well Mark wouldn't remember to tell me anything. Unless he wanted me to do something for him." He covered his eyes with an unsteady hand for a moment. "It drops right back in our laps, doesn't it?"

"How do you mean?" Quist asked.

"If the Tiptoe boy is innocent." Jerry opened his eyes and a bitter smile flickered at the corner of his mouth. "Where was I at the moment Caroline was killed? Is that what comes next?"

"Routine," Kreevich said.

"I was here," Jerry said. "I was a little potted—got that way listening to Tommy Bayne's night with Noel Coward, and watching Miriam Talbot rub her bosoms against Mark.

She should have been more discreet, don't you think?"

"On the make," Quist said.

Jerry laughed. "She made it long ago," he said. "Or didn't you know? Good old, faithful old Mark has been making out with her for months in hotels, motels, and Miriam's pink satin apartment in New York."

"An affair?" Kreevich asked.

"A running orgy," Jerry said. "No harm in telling you, now that Caroline isn't here to hear it. Poor dear Caroline, she never had the slightest notion of it. She used to laugh at Miriam's sexy attempts at Mark. She felt so secure!"

"If it was so well known, others must have been covering for Mark, too," Quist said. Anger was stirring in him. Mark's pious double talk!

"Pat Grant, of course. Beatrice, of course. Tommy Bayne helped engineer many of the assignations. Mark had only to go down the road three miles to Tommy's cottage if there was no time for something more elaborate."

"I thought Miriam was Bayne's girl," Quist said.

"My dear Julian, Tommy hasn't been interested in girls since age four, when he played 'doctor' with one of them under his front porch and found they weren't as attractive as boys."

"Did the Talbot girl resent Mrs. Stillwell?" Kreevich asked.

"Why should she resent her? She had her man. She could tap Mark for all the money she needed. Caroline was a source of amusement to her. While everyone thought Caroline was the greatest, Miriam knew she'd outsexed her, outmaneuvered her, outgeneraled her."

"And you just watched and let it happen?" Quist asked.

"What the hell was I to do, wreck Caroline's life for her?

As long as she had no doubts about Mark, I wasn't going to smash things to pieces for her."

"Or have Mark cut off the money you needed from him," Quist said.

Jerry looked at Quist quite steadily. "Why do you think I stayed here and put up with Mark's treatment? When the roof caved in on Caroline, somebody had to be here to help her." He drew a deep breath. "I loved her, if it matters. You ask, why didn't I tell her about Mark and make my own play for her?"

"Consider it asked."

"Because she was a one-man woman! Because she'd have forgiven him if he'd asked for it. Because nobody was ever going to matter to her but that sonofabitch brother of mine."

Jerry took a deep drag on his cigarette and was silent.

"Back to routine," Kreevich said. "You came down here, a little drunk, when the party broke up last night. You can't see the pool area from here, can you?"

"No."

"You went to bed?"

"No."

"What, then?"

"An evening like that—Miriam playing public games with Mark, Lewis eyeing all the women except his wife, believing he could buy any one of them if he chose—left me up-tight. I didn't think I could sleep—without maybe another drink or two. So I had a drink or two—considered the possibility of burning all my paintings—" Again the bitter smile. "Then I heard the police siren."

"But you didn't come over to the pool," Quist said. "I don't recall seeing you there or up at the house later."

"I started to go," Jerry said. "The main entrance is just off to the left there. I'd only gone a few yards when I saw a jalopy parked there. I figured a patrolling trooper had seen it and come in to find the driver. So let him do the job, I told myself, and I came back here and went to bed. And to sleep."

"When did you know what had really happened?"

"When Shallert brought that Captain Jadwin down to ask me questions."

"You told Jadwin what you've told us?" Kreevich asked.

"Perhaps not so colorfully—but yes."

Kreevich hesitated. "Jadwin was shot to death in Grand Central Station late this morning."

Jerry just stared at him.

"Was Shallert here while Jadwin questioned you?" Kreevich asked.

"No. I assume he went back to the house."

"Did you go to find Mark—to commiserate with him, see if you could do anything to help?" Quist asked.

"No," Jerry said, his voice harsh. "I had no stomach to watch his phony grieving. There was nothing I could do to help Caroline, the only person I cared for. Jadwin told me they'd caught the murderer. Damn good young folk singer named Johnny Tiptoe. I used to go down to the Boat Club to listen to him. It was hard to think he could have hurt Caroline."

"We don't think he did," Kreevich said.

"Who, then?"

Kreevich didn't answer the question. "Can you guess why Mrs. Stillwell came down to the pool? She wasn't dressed for swimming. It's as if she saw something that brought her down there in a hurry, without stopping to change slippers that were ruined by the wet grass."

Jerry shook his head slowly. "I can't guess."

Kreevich seemed to have run out of questions, but then he came up with one more. "Did Mrs. Stillwell know you were in love with her, Jerry?"

Jerry looked down at his hands, which weren't quite steady. "Not because I told her," he said, "because I never did. It was enough for me, because I knew there was nothing else, that she was obviously fond of me. Perhaps she knew, because she was a sensitive person. She kept trying to persuade me to take my paintings to New York, find myself a gallery—go it on my own."

"Why didn't you?" Quist asked. "Your paintings are damn good."

"I pretended I didn't think so. I pretended I didn't have any confidence in them." He looked up at Quist. "You see, I didn't want to leave her—in case she might need me." His mouth tightened. "You can be sure I'll be out of here now, just as soon as I can pack and go."

"No one is going anywhere just yet," Kreevich said.

It was a little after four o'clock when Quist got back to the city. There was nothing more he could do to help Kreevich at the Stillwell place. He garaged his car and went to his office.

Gloria Chard, the receptionist, gave Quist her enchanting smile. "We grow old when you're not here, boss," she said. "People don't believe it when we say you're out. They're convinced you're hiding somewhere in the back."

"Anyone important?" Quist asked.

"No one who can't wait. Anything new where you've been?"

"Private dirt—but no evidence," Quist said.

Quist walked along the rear corridor to his office. As always, Connie Parmalee was waiting for him, her eyes shaded by her tinted granny glasses.

"You look as if you could use a drink," she said.

"I could," Quist said. As he sat down in his desk chair, he realized he ached all over. He hadn't slept since the night before last.

Miss Parmalee went to the bar in the corner of the office and poured Quist a deep slug of bourbon on the rocks. He drank a part of it gratefully. "Will you tell Lydia I'm back, Connie."

"She hasn't come in all day," Connie said. "I guess your murder was a little much for her."

"Then she doesn't know about Jadwin?"

"She does if she's listened to the radio or watched her TV set," Connie said. "It's also in the evening *Post*."

"Call her, will you, doll?"

He reached for one of his long, thin cigars, kept in a cedar-lined box on his desk. He would check in with Lydia and go to his apartment for a spot of shuteye. He couldn't think any more; didn't want to think any more. Kreevich was a good man. He'd come up with answers. He took another sip of his drink and closed his eyes.

"Lydia doesn't answer at her place," Connie said.

"Try her at mine," Quist said. "The usual signal."

Lydia, who had a key to his place, wouldn't answer the phone there without a special way of calling. He would let the phone ring just twice, hang up, and then call again. Connie knew the system. She dialed, hung up, and then dialed again. After a long wait she reported no answer.

"I'm going home and get some sleep," Quist said. "When

she checks in, tell her. I can't keep my eyes open."

He took a cab to his apartment, though it was only about six blocks. It seemed to take an insuperable effort to get upstairs and into his place, where the late afternoon sun was pouring in from the terrace. He stopped by the telephone on the long stretcher table in the center of the room. If Lydia, who had a key to the apartment, had been here and given up waiting for him, she might have left a message on the pad by the phone. There was nothing.

He stumbled up the stairs to the second floor of his duplex, took off his clothes, scattering them on the chairs in his dressing room, and went into the bathroom. He stood for a few moments under a steaming hot shower, then dried himself and felt his way, like a blind man, to the king-size bed in his bedroom, pausing for an instant to close the Venetian blinds at the windows to shut out the light. He was gone the instant his head hit the pillow.

How much later, he didn't know at first, Quist swam back to a sort of half consciousness. Without thinking, he reached out in the dark and found, disappointingly, that he was alone in the bed. He turned his head to look at the illuminated dial of his bedside clock. It was almost midnight. He had slept for a solid seven hours.

He turned on the lamp and lay back against his pillow, deliciously relaxed. The day behind him came into focus —a day of violence and horror. Then he thought that Lydia had left him alone because she knew how badly he needed rest and sleep. He picked up the phone on the side table and dialed her number. It rang for a long time without any response. He put down the phone and lay there on his bed, frowning, for a moment or two. Then he got up, slipped into a dressing gown, and went downstairs to his living room, turning on lights as he went.

In a drawer of the table on which the phone rested was a small address book. He looked up Gloria Chard's home number and dialed it. His glamorous receptionist answered after three rings.

"The boss here," Quist said. "Sorry to call you so late, Gloria."

"It's just the shank of the evening," Gloria said.

"Didn't Lydia ever come into the office this afternoon?"

"No, boss."

"She didn't leave any message for me?"

"Not that I got."

"I don't seem to be able to locate her."

Gloria sounded hopeful. "Maybe you have a rival, boss," she said.

"Drop dead," Quist said cheerfully.

He called Dan Garvey at home. Garvey sounded as though he might not be alone. He hadn't seen or heard from Lydia all day. Quist put down the phone and lit one of his long, thin cigars. It had been some time since he hadn't known where to reach Lydia when he wanted her. Office in the daytime, and with him almost all of their free time. On the rare occasion when she went somewhere with other people, he knew exactly who they were and where they would be. She must have been curious about his day, and yet not curious enough to call him and ask him about it.

He found himself fantasying disasters—a hit-and-run driver, a mugger, a rapist with a knife! He remembered a psychiatrist friend telling him that fantasies of that sort were really an outlet for anger. He was hoping Lydia would be punished for not being in touch.

So, let there be a little reality in this. Something could have happened to her; she could be ill; there could, really, have been an accident. They lived in a violent city.

Quist went back upstairs, dressed himself in a dark blue tropical worsted summer suit and a lighter blue turtle-neck shirt. He went down in the elevator and out into the soft summer night. It was only two blocks to Lydia's apartment —two brightly lighted blocks. Off to his left he heard the eerie sound of a tugboat whistle on the river.

The night doorman at Lydia's building knew him. He hadn't seen Lydia since he'd come on duty at eight o'clock. They tried the house phone. No answer.

Quist went up to the fourth floor and let himself into Lydia's apartment. He had a key, just as she had a key to his place. Lydia wasn't at home. The apartment was in apple pie order. He went to the closet in her bedroom and looked at the row of dresses and coats hanging there. He couldn't remember what she'd been wearing when he'd brought her home that morning; he couldn't guess what was missing. Being a mere male, he couldn't be sure what things she kept here and what things she kept at his place.

He went back to her living room and wrote a note which he propped against the phone.

Phone me when you get in if you don't want to be drawn and quartered. Luv. Q.

He left, reluctantly, thinking he must have overlooked something that would make everything obvious. He walked back to his apartment, now imagining that she would be there, waiting for him.

She wasn't.

He was aware of a faint chill of alarm spreading over his body. People who knew that he and Lydia were, in effect, living together probably thought of it as a kind of glamorous romp. It was much more than that. They were so close, so deeply in love, that even a few hours of enforced separation was a cause of pain to both of them. They played no games with each other. It was inconceivable that Lydia would vanish for more than twelve hours without letting him know where she was and why. She wouldn't "forget" to call. It was the complete trust, the mutual need for each other, that made Lydia's unexplained absence, without word, frightening.

From somewhere, long ago, Quist had acquired Lieutenant Kreevich's private phone number. He called it. Kreevich answered, sounding sleepy.

"Julian Quist here," Quist said. "I'm sorry to bother you at this time of night."

"It's the curse of being a cop," Kreevich said. "Something new? Damn little turned up at Stillwell's place."

"I think you know something about my relationship with Lydia Morton," Quist said.

"And envy you for it."

"I brought her home from the Stillwells' yesterday morning and dropped her at her apartment about nine-thirty. Later I went back out to Stillwell's with you. Lydia never checked in at the office during the day. I've heard nothing from her since I got back. She isn't at her place. She hasn't been here. If you know about us, you know this isn't normal."

"Why have you called me?" Kreevich asked.

"Because the police aren't going to be too concerned about someone who hasn't checked in with what they'd call her 'boy friend' for less than a day. I thought you'd know who to call who'd give me a quick check on accidents, muggings, anything that might account for Lydia's silence."

"Can do." Kreevich's voice had gone hard. "Is that really why you called me?"

"Why else?"

"Your subconscious telling you this may have something to do with the Stillwell case?"

"Why, for God sake?"

"Pressure on you to get out of the act."

Quist's mouth had gone dry. "Wouldn't I have been warned, threatened?"

"Do you have to have the message spelled out for you?"

Quist drew a painful breath. "You think that may be it?"

"I don't know what I think—yet," Kreevich said. "I'll get an accident-crime report for you as soon as I can. You'll be at your place?"

"Unless I hear from Lydia."

"Let me know if you do. It may take a couple of hours to get the report you want."

"Kreevich?"

"Yes?"

Quist's hand was gripping the phone so hard it hurt. "Why am I dangerous to—to whoever it is?"

"Because you're a persistent bastard," Kreevich said. "Let's hope we're dreaming."

chapter 2

Nothing from Lydia.

About a quarter to four in the morning Quist's phone rang. It was Kreevich.

"No accident or crime reported that would appear to involve Miss Morton," he said. "Hospitals negative; morgue negative, if you consider that encouraging. Nothing on any police blotter that would indicate any young, handsome woman was in any kind of trouble. Let me ask you a painful question. You had no falling-out with Miss Morton, no quarrel?"

"For Christ sake, no! Lydia and I are—we're one person!"

"Not just a temporary squabble for which she could be punishing you?"

"We're not a miserable, backbiting, married couple!" Quist said.

"I just thought I'd ask. Because—"

"Because what?"

"Because I don't like to think she's in the hands of the same kind of butcher who did for Mrs. Stillwell," Kreevich said. "I'm coming over to see you. Stay put."

Quist walked over to the bar and poured himself a straight slug of bourbon. He felt cold—his hands, his feet, his heart. Just a little more than twenty-four hours ago Caroline had walked down to the pool and been hacked to death. He, Quist, had been responsible for clearing Johnny Tiptoe and turning the cops in the direction of the Stillwell family and their friends. Jadwin had been stopped in his tracks when he followed that lead. David Lewis or Mark Stillwell could sit on their behinds in the country and hire the muscle to do the stopping. They could hire the muscle that would make Lydia disappear. But to what end?

Kreevich arrived in less than half an hour. He looked grim.

"I've been trying to make sense out of this," he said. "You're a rich man. Not Stillwell-rich, but well off. Your relationship with Miss Morton is no secret. It could be a simple kidnaping."

"Simple?"

"I mean not connected with the Stillwell thing at all. If it is, you'll get some kind of demand for ransom."

"I hope to God that's what it is," Quist said.

"Maybe we're too Stillwell-conscious," Kreevich said. "But you did point at them by clearing Tiptoe. You did announce, pretty publicly, that Caroline was your friend and you were going to get the sonofabitch that killed her. You gave the cops all they have to work on at the moment. You were riding tandem with me yesterday morning. You could look dangerous to them."

96

"More dangerous than the police?"

"You were an old friend of Caroline Stillwell's. Knew her before she was married and was Caroline Cummings, the movie star. You might know something about her that could point at someone."

"But I don't!"

"The killer doesn't know that you don't—if there is such a thing. You have to be stopped. Lydia is missing, so you've got the message. You go back to work today, tend to your own knitting, make it clear you've dropped the case. Then, maybe—"

"And if that isn't it?"

"I don't like to think of the alternative," Kreevich said.

"What alternative?"

"Revenge," Kreevich said in a cold voice. "We have to think we're dealing with some kind of psychotic, the way Mrs. Stillwell was mutilated. That kind of person might want to get even with you for screwing things up for him."

"Jesus!"

"We've overlooked one thing, Julian. There's a head-shrinker involved in the case—Dr. Frankel who got a call from someone in the Stillwell house. Plush Park Avenue address. I suggest we go see him."

"At five o'clock in the morning?"

"What's good enough for us is good enough for him. Do you want to waste time being polite?"

Dr. Milton Frankel was a big man; big-boned, pallid, little crow's-feet of worry at the corners of wide brown, almost innocent eyes. The doorman at his building refused to communicate until he got a look at Kreevich's shield. Dr. Frankel greeted them, wearing a cotton dressing gown over pale blue pajamas. He looked at Kreevich's credentials and acknowledged an introduction to Quist with a curt nod of his big head.

"This is a pretty extraordinary time of day for a call, Lieutenant," he said. His voice was deep, gentle, trained, Quist thought, never to be critical—part of the technique of his business.

They found themselves in what must have been the waiting room of the doctor's office—four Windsor chairs, a table loaded down with current magazines, two cubist paintings on the wall, glass ash trays from the dime store. Frankel didn't waste money on his waiting room décor.

Frankel indicated chairs, and then perched on the edge of the table himself. It left him, Quist saw, looking down at his visitors, an old police trick.

"I can only suppose some patient of mine has gotten himself into trouble," Frankel said. "I have to tell you in advance, Lieutenant, I can't discuss the clinical aspects of any patient's case."

"About three o'clock yesterday morning you had a phone call, Doctor," Kreevich said.

"Did I?"

"It was an out-of-area call. We have a record of it."

"So?"

"Who made that call to you, Doctor?"

The doctor's eyes narrowed. He reached in his dressing gown pocket for a cigarette and lit it. "You don't know?" he asked Kreevich.

"Or I wouldn't ask you the question," Kreevich said. "I know where the call was made from, but not who made it."

"Where was it made from?"

"Mark Stillwell's home in Westchester."

"So that's it," Frankel said. "I read an account of the murder of Mrs. Stillwell in last night's paper. Also a policeman? An unhappy business."

"So who called you, Doctor?"

Frankel took a deep drag on his cigarette and let the smoke out slowly in a curling spiral toward the ceiling. "There are certain ethics in my business, Lieutenant. I do not reveal the identity of my patients. There is a stupid prejudice against people who are undergoing psychiatric treatment. The general public, even their friends and relatives, assume that the patient is off his rocker. Neurosis is not a symptom of insanity. I treat neurotics, not psychotics. You know the difference, Lieutenant?"

"I know the difference."

"Analysis doesn't work with psychotics," Frankel said.

"The technical lecture would be interesting at some other time," Kreevich said. "Right now I need to know who called you from the Stillwell home."

Frankel studied the end of his cigarette. "If you knew who called me, I would admit it," he said. "But to reveal that identity to you would be to breach a confidence. The person would no longer trust me and I would lose my effectiveness as a therapist."

"We have two, possibly three murders on our hands," Kreevich said. He heard Quist's sharp intake of breath but he didn't look away from Frankel. "It could go on—a chain reaction. Are you willing to have that on your conscience, Doctor?"

"Do you think someone at the Stillwells'—someone there at the time Mrs. Stillwell was killed, also shot your fellow police officer?"

"Or had him killed," Kreevich said.

Frankel put out his half-smoked cigarette. "If I were asked to testify as to the legal sanity—or insanity—of a patient, I would. But to reveal that patient's identity in advance of due process— I'm sorry."

"You are beginning to bore me, Doctor," Quist said, his voice not quite steady. "Surely you must know that the Lieutenant can go through the laborious business of checking out on everyone, and today, tomorrow, next week he'll know who your patient is."

"Will a little delay make that much difference?" Frankel asked.

Quist stood up and confronted the doctor. He was looking down now. "Enough to justify my cutting out your heart, Frankel," he said.

"Easy," Kreevich said.

"A person very dear to me has disappeared," Quist said. "That disappearance may have been arranged by your patient. My friend may have been tortured, killed, by the time you decide to tell us what we need to know now—not later today or next week. If that happens because of you, I promise—I promise you will wish you had never been born."

"I don't think I care to listen to threats," Frankel said. "But—I will tell you this much, Mr. Quist. The person who called me on the phone is not capable of the kind of crimes that have been committed, or may be committed."

"Then why did he call you?"

"For help," Frankel said, without hesitation. "The relationship between analyst and patient is a very special one. While the analysis is in progress, the patient becomes enormously dependent on the doctor. In any kind of crisis he calls for help. He needs to know that the doctor is there, available."

"If your patient wasn't responsible for the violence that took place at the Stillwells', why did he need your reassurance?" Kreevich asked.

"Guilt is a peculiar thing as it works in the subconscious," Frankel said. "A man could be jealous of a woman, or desire a woman who belongs to somebody else, or hate a woman because she had turned him down, denigrated his feeling of manhood. Then something violent happens to her. He feels guilty because subconsciously he had wanted her punished. If he's in analysis, he might call his doctor to be reassured that he is not guilty."

"Is that what happened?"

"Hypothetical case," Frankel said, fishing for another cigarette.

Quist turned away and headed for the door. He turned. "If delay costs us another life, Frankel, I promise you the need to punish you will not be in my subconscious."

Seven A.M.

There was no word from Lydia, no word from anyone about Lydia. Fear for her began to beat inside Quist like a painful pulse. There was no one to turn to, no one to ask about Lydia who knew as much about her as he did himself. He knew every intimate detail of her life, her past, her friends, her habits.

At a little after seven, back in his apartment, Quist called Dan Garvey. Garvey sounded sleepy and grouchy.

"I'm sorry to disturb you, Daniel," Quist said. "Apologize to the lady, if there is one there."

Garvey told him what he could go do to himself.

"There's no word from Lydia, Dan. Nothing. She's just disappeared into thin air."

"No possible slip-up on a message?" Garvey asked. He

sounded more awake.

"I don't think so."

"Who was on the reception desk when Gloria went to lunch yesterday?"

"Don't know."

"Gloria wouldn't slip up," Garvey said, "but her luncheon replacement might. You're sure Lydia didn't leave a message for you in your apartment?"

"Positive."

"Maybe she didn't anchor it properly and it blew out the window. You looked on the terrace—tangled up in one of the shrubs out there?"

"I haven't looked. I will—now."

"There's always a perfectly normal explanation for this kind of thing. There's been a failure in communication that Lydia couldn't have anticipated."

"But where could she have been all night?"

"A sick relative," Garvey said. "Put on some coffee. I'll be over there in twenty minutes. And cheer up. We'll find a rational answer to this, you'll see."

Quist went out onto the terrace, feeling a faint glimmer of hope. The terrace doors had been open all yesterday. It was August. A written message just might have blown away.

If it had, it was no longer on the terrace.

Quist went back to the phone and called Gloria Chard's home phone. His glamorous receptionist answered on the second ring.

"I hoped you'd be up," Quist said. "Who took your place at the reception desk when you went out to lunch yesterday?"

"No one," Goria said. "I didn't go out. Why?"

"Lydia," Quist said, feeling his small hope fading. "There's been no word from her since yesterday morning when I dropped her at her apartment. I thought it was possible, while you were out for lunch, that somebody might have screwed up a message I should have gotten."

"I didn't go out, boss. Things were pretty hectic with you and Lydia both out of the office. I just had coffee. Good for my measurements."

"Your measurements don't need help," Quist said. "There was no message from Lydia?"

"She didn't come in or check in all day," Gloria said. "You're worried, aren't you? Have you tried—?"

"Hospitals, police—yes."

"What can I do?"

"Just hold down your desk this morning and make sure any kind of message for me, no matter how screwy, gets to me at once. Any kind of strange creep insists on seeing me, don't turn him off. I'll see him."

"You think—?"

"I don't know what I think, Gloria, except that I'm frightened for Lydia."

Garvey arrived a moment or two later. He didn't have to ask Quist if anything "rational" had turned up. Tension was written in every line of Quist's face, in his usually relaxed body. Garvey went into the kitchenette and poured himself some coffee. He came back, balancing the cup and saucer in the palm of his hand.

"What do you really think is behind this, Julian?"

Quist told him. "It's a message to me to get out of the act."

"So get out," Garvey said.

"And what happens to Lydia?"

"When they're sure you've backed off, they turn her loose."

"And she tells us who's been holding her? How can they turn her loose, now or any other time, Daniel?"

Garvey scowled down at his precariously balanced coffee cup. Quist, pale, his bright blue eyes blazing out of dark holes in his face, suddenly pounded the arm of his chair.

"You ever asked yourself if you could kill a man for personal reasons?" he asked. "Because if they have done away with Lydia, I'll have just one aim left in life, Daniel. I'll wipe out the whole miserable mob of them, guilty or innocent."

"Knock it off!" Garvey said. He put down his coffee cup and lit a cigarette. "Make you feel better to shout threats into the wind, go ahead. When you're finished, let's try to make sense."

"You think I don't mean it?" Quist said. "There isn't anything worth saving if Lydia is gone."

"It might be worth trying to think the way they are thinking," Garvey said.

"How the hell can you think the way they think? We don't, for Christ sake, know who we're trying to think like!"

"You may still get some kind of a ransom demand," Garvey said. "Meanwhile, let's try to think it through. You want to go on shouting threats I'll go somewhere else and think."

Quist covered his face with his hands for a moment—unsteady hands. "I'm sorry, Daniel," he said in a low, shaken voice.

"Don't be sorry," Garvey said. "If we have to kill people, I'll help you! But first, let's try to add things up." He put

104

out his half-smoked cigarette and lit another one. "We have to guess that someone in the Stillwell household night before last knows who killed Caroline. They had a lucky break. Tiptoe appeared on the scene and almost saved the day for them by looking guilty. You blew that out for them. You convinced Jadwin. What was the point in killing him? You'd just pass on what you knew to somebody else. You did just that. You also announced, loud and clear, that Caroline was your friend and you were going to get her killer. But you've told what you know to the cops. Why try to silence you now?"

"Revenge, God help us!" Quist said.

"There's one thing missing to make that hold up a hundred percent, Julian. If we're dealing with a crazy psychotic who wants to pay you back, wouldn't he want you to know exactly why he's grabbed Lydia? You'd have had a phone call, a note, letting you know you'd been paid off."

"I don't have to be told. Lydia's absence tells me."

"Maybe not," Garvey said. "Let's pretend for a minute we're dealing with a very cool customer who's not interested in revenge at all. What did Jadwin's murder get him? What does Lydia's disappearance get him? It gets him time, Julian. The police are looking for Jadwin's killer more urgently than they are Caroline's, because they think it's the same person. They turn you off by taking Lydia. It gets our man time!"

"Time for what?"

"To wipe out anything that would connect him with Caroline's murder. One or two other lives don't matter, as long as they can't be charged to him. And let's look at it, dad. No one in that household killed Jadwin. All accounted for that morning—Mark, Jerry, Mrs. Lorimer, the Lewises,

Patrick Grant. None of them in Grand Central Station. So if one of them killed Caroline, the same person didn't kill Jadwin."

"You're saying it was a coincidence? Someone unrelated to the Stillwell murder just happened to kill Jadwin?"

"No," Garvey said, "and I'm not thinking it. There are four people, however, that we don't know about, pal. We don't know about Tommy Bayne, your Noel Coward kid, or Mark's mistress, the Talbot girl. We don't know about Dr. Frankel. And we don't know about Lewis's lawyer, Max Gottfried, who got three phone calls from Lewis in the middle of the night. Bayne and Miriam Talbot went home, we think, after the party. Frankel we know, from the phone call to him, was in New York. Ditto Gottfried. We assume none of them murdered Caroline. Bayne and the Talbot girl need checking out, but the two men we know were in New York."

"So?"

"Muscle," Garvey said. "I mentioned it before— yesterday morning. David Lewis and Mark Stillwell can buy muscle, would know where to buy it. Patrick Grant, too, for that matter. Any one of them if you want to leave the door open, but I like Lewis or Mark. So they turned their muscle loose on Jadwin, and then they turned it loose on you—through Lydia. While we blow our minds about Lydia, they gain time to whitewash the first killer."

"A fascinating theory," Quist said, "but what the hell do we do?"

"We find a way to apply our own heat," Garvey said.

Under normal conditions the offices of Julian Quist Associates have an atmosphere of gaiety and good cheer; it's part of what they have to sell. There are the mod paintings, the bright colors, the beautiful girls on the staff wearing beautiful clothes, the ordinarily electric excitement generated by Quist himself, that contribute to making a visit there an unusual adventure.

At about ten o'clock on the morning after Lydia's disappearance the gathering in Quist's private office was a long way from being cheerful. Quist sat at his desk, his eyes hollowed out, his mouth a straight, hard slit in his face. Connie Parmalee, mini-skirted, had brought him coffee which he didn't touch. She hovered close to him, her tinted granny glasses hiding the anxiety in her hazel eyes. The glamorous Gloria Chard had been relieved of her duties at the reception desk and was sitting on a modern love seat with Bobby Hilliard, whose boyish face was puckered with concern. Garvey prowled the office, talking. He had put the whole story, in all its details, to these trusted people.

"Julian, on the surface, has got to play this as though he was following their unspoken orders. He will stay here during office hours; business as usual. God knows who is watching or who may be watching. He will see clients who should be seen, he will make it easy for them to see that he's backed away, is doing nothing to interfere with them."

Quist made a groaning noise. Connie reached out a hand to him, but withdrew it before it touched him.

"The rest of us have jobs to do, and we have to do them as cleverly as we have ever done anything in our lives."

"Anything at all," Bobby Hilliard said. "But what, Dan? What can we do that won't be obviously working for Julian?"

"What are we looking for?" Garvey said, his frown dark. "We're looking for what I call muscle. We're looking for a whole scene that's being covered up at the Stillwell place. The more I think about it, the more I think there is a conspiracy to hide the facts about Caroline's murder. I think that more than one person is involved in covering for the murderer. Have you looked at this morning's paper, Julian?"

Quist raised dead eyes to his friend. The paper was lying on his desk, but he hadn't glanced at it. If he had, he'd have seen that Connie had marked a front-page article in red pencil. It was standard office practice. Anything in the news that had anything to do with one of their many clients was marked for Quist so that he didn't have to go hunting.

Garvey pointed at the paper, and Quist looked down at it.

MARK STILLWELL TO HEAD SPORTS COMPLEX

David Lewis announced today that Mark Stillwell, head of Stillwell Enterprises, will be President and General Manager of the great new Sports Complex being financed by Lewis interests, construction of which is to begin this month. David Lewis announced he had made the choice of Stillwell after considering several candidates. Unfortunately, Mr. Stillwell was not available for comment because of the tragic murder of his wife at their Westchester home yesterday morning. Mr. Lewis said that he had not withheld the announcement because "in this tragic time I felt it should be quite clear that I have complete faith and confidence in Mark Stillwell. . . ."

Quist looked up. "This is the job Mark was so concerned about," he said. "A strange time for Lewis to announce it.

Unless, of course, he'd released it before—"

"No," Garvey said. " 'In this tragic time I felt it should be quite clear—' Released after the murder. Why the hurry? Whatever the reason—and it could be that he needs Mark's support—it's opened the door for us. We have a contract to handle the public relations for the Sports Complex. With this announcement made without consulting us, we have a reason to go straight to the horse's mouth for information, without seeming to be prying into the murder case."

"The main reason we got the contract," Connie said, "is your past reputation in the world of sports, Dan. The Sports Complex is your baby."

"Which makes Lewis my baby." Garvey lit a cigarette. "A dangerous link in their chain, friends, is Miriam Talbot. If Mark is having an affair with her, as Jerry Stillwell told Julian, she could hurt Mark badly, if she chose. Lewis would want that relationship kept quiet for business reasons, and Mark would want it kept quiet because it might appear to give him a motive for killing his wife. Miss Talbot is dynamite."

"And she won't open her mouth because she knows how much her silence is worth," Quist said.

Garvey's mouth moved in a wry smile. "She will also have to stay away from Mark for a while. Now a nice young man who watched her twirling her boobs around at the Stillwell party might be overcome with a passionate desire for her."

"Oh, no!" Bobby Hilliard said. "She's a man-eater!"

"Should be a fascinating new experience for you, son," Garvey said. "You don't need an introduction. She may need someone to play games with while Mark is in mourning. She's your pigeon, Robert."

"Oh, God!" Bobby said.

"And since we're using sex as a weapon—" Garvey said, turning his eyes to Gloria Chard.

"Who do I get, the chauffeur?" Miss Chard asked.

"You get Patrick Grant, who, from all accounts, is a dreamboat," Garvey said. "We can't talk to Mark in this 'tragic time.' But since the news of Mark's job has been released, Julian Quist Associates have to know what the score is. What line are we to follow during this 'tragic time'?"

"And who do I get?" Connie Parmalee asked, looking demurely down at her lovely legs. "The chauffeur, the houseman?"

"You get two enigmas, love," Garvey said. "Not the two you mentioned, however. Have you been feeling well lately?"

"I feel fine," Connie said, surprised.

"I thought I detected symptoms of depression," Garvey said, his smile widening. "You haven't been sleeping well, have you?"

"I've been sleeping alone, if that answers your question," Connie said.

"Pressures of your job, secretary to a high-powered executive, getting you down?"

"Stop kidding, Daniel!"

"I just thought you might need a little psychiatric help," Garvey said. "We know a very good Park Avenue man, name of Frankel."

"Oh," Connie said.

"You can invent your own symptoms," Garvey said. "What I'm interested in is where he keeps his case records. We might have to do a little housebreaking sooner or later."

"And my second love interest?" Connie asked.

"Mr. Max Gottfried, Lewis's lawyer. Because of this

'tragic time,' Julian Quist Associates hesitate to go to the principals—Lewis and Mark. It would be logical to inquire of Mr. Gottfried just what line we should be following." Garvey put out his cigarette. "You're all to watch for the smallest kind of thing—the batting of an eyelid, the smallest hesitation when the subject of the murder comes up. It would naturally come up, you know. Any questions?"

Quist was looking down at his desk top with blank eyes. "You've left out one very important person who may have a lot of answers, Daniel," he said.

"I know," Garvey said. "I haven't figured out yet just how we get to Beatrice Lorimer."

The phone light blinked on Quist's desk, and Connie picked up. She listened, and then looked at Garvey. "You can cross out one of my victims," she said. "Mr. Max Gottfried is here to see Julian."

Quist sat bolt upright in his chair, his eyes taking on light. It was just possible Lewis's lawyer might be here to bargain for Lydia; indirectly, but bargain.

The staff had left the office, and Quist was leaning back in his chair, smoking one of his long, thin cigars, and looking quite relaxed when Connie ushered in Mr. Max Gottfried. The lawyer was a short, almost strikingly ugly man. His head was too big for his body, covered by a mane of thick black hair, styled Edwardian, with sideburns that were almost mutton-chop whiskers. He had a great beak of a nose, flanked at the top by bushy black eyebrows. His eyes were bright and as cold as two newly minted dimes. Quist had the uncomfortable feeling that those eyes were trained from long courtroom and legal experience to read through any kind of sham or game playing. Leathery-looking skin

111

was stretched tight over high cheekbones and a bony jaw, as if the man's skull was trying to force its way out. He was dressed in a plain but obviously expensive charcoal gray, summer-weight suit, a white button-down shirt and a black, crocheted silk tie.

Gottfried walked past Connie in the doorway and stood looking at Quist, reading him, studying him, his red-lipped mouth a slightly crooked gash in his face. Quist rose from his chair, trying to show nothing but polite curiosity.

Then Gottfried smiled. It was an unexpectedly warm, almost paternal smile.

"Thank you for seeing me so promptly, Mr. Quist," he said.

"Do come in and sit down," Quist said. "As a matter of fact, I should have been calling you if you hadn't come here."

"Why?" Gottfried asked, still smiling.

To ask you what you and your friends have done with Lydia, you sonofabitch! That was what Quist wanted to say. But he was returning Gottfried's smile, gesturing to a chair.

"Cigar? Is it too early in the day for a drink?" he asked. He glanced at the intercom box on his desk. He had switched it on so that Garvey and the others could listen in.

"Thanks, but I don't smoke or drink," Gottfried said. "In my business there isn't an hour round the clock when I don't have to be ready for some kind of crisis."

Like three calls from Lewis in the early hours of yesterday morning.

Gottfried sat down in an armchair facing Quist. "You say you were on the point of calling me, Mr. Quist." He had chosen to make a small advantage for himself.

112

Quist picked up the newspaper on his desk. "This announcement about Mark Stillwell's appointment," he said.

"You object?" Gottfried asked, still smiling.

"I don't object to the appointment," Quist said. "Why should I? Mark is a friend of mine. His wife was an old friend. I wish him well. I have a deep sympathy for him at this moment."

"An altogether ghastly situation," Gottfried said. His smile faded and the bright eyes seemed to bore into Quist. "Dave Lewis felt it was an appropriate time to show his public support. Is that what you object to, Mr. Quist?"

Quist knocked the ash off the end of his cigar. "You keep using the word 'object,' Mr. Gottfried. I haven't said I objected to anything. I was going to call you to set up some kind of ground rules."

"Ground rules for what?"

"You wouldn't be here if you weren't aware that my firm has signed a contract to handle the public relations for the Sports Complex for the next four years." Or would you? Have you just come here to find out how I am reacting to Lydia's disappearance? "If we are to do an effective job for you, Mr. Gottfried, we can't have press releases going out that we aren't aware of and haven't approved of in advance, even if they come from the top man."

"Meaning Dave Lewis?"

"Yes, or anyone else."

"Then you don't think that announcement should have been released?"

"I don't think it should have been released without our knowing ahead of time."

"If you had been asked, would you have agreed to have it released?"

"No. I would have advised against it."

"So you do object," Gottfried said, his smile reappearing.

"If that word is all that will satisfy you."

"So perhaps you will tell me why," Gottfried said.

Quist put down his cigar. He was fighting the urge to take this man by the throat and choke the truth out of him. He kept his hands out of sight because he was afraid they were shaking.

"The man who heads up the Sports Complex has to have a very careful image built for him," Quist said. "Mark has many of the right elements—good-looking, not too old, athletic, rich, and, up to yesterday, happy. The Sports Complex represents a pleasure climate. The millions of people who will go to it when it's built are concerned only with fun and games. The man who heads it has to be someone who appears also to be concerned with fun and games. Someone they can identify with. Mark could be it—but somewhat later, Mr. Gottfried. Fun lovers are not going to be attracted to a mourner, a man in the center of a sexual violence, a man who—"

"Sexual violence?" Gottfried cut in sharply.

A nerve twitched in Quist's cheek. "I saw Caroline as the murderer left her," he said. "Her underthings had been ripped off, her breasts and her stomach slashed and re-slashed. Only some kind of a sex-oriented lunatic would have taken time to mutilate her in that fashion. It could have been a brutal attempt at rape."

"I hadn't gotten that impression," Gottfried said without emotion.

"I saw her!" Quist fought to keep his voice level. "The man we're publicizing for a fun job shouldn't be involved in such a situation. That's all anybody is going to associate

114

with him just now. A month from now, when the case is closed and the murderer behind bars, the public will have forgotten. There will be new murders, new scandals. Right now there are people who may even suspect him—until the real murderer is caught. Not a good image."

Gottfried crossed one leg over the other. He ran a finger down one side of his big nose. "I agree with you a hundred percent," he said. "That's why I'm here."

"So you object, too."

"To put it mildly," Gottfried said. "So we're faced with a problem."

"We?"

"We have to counter the damage that release can do Mark Stillwell. We have to build sympathy for him, at the same time slipping in all the information we can that makes it clear he's the right man for the Sports Complex job. How do you go about it?"

"It's not an overnight job," Quist said. "We have to go about it carefully, watching every move that's made until the murder is solved. When a decent interval has passed, we get him seen at sporting events—football games, hockey games, the professional golf tour when it begins in the winter."

"But right now we need to build sympathy for him," Gottfried said. "A feature article, perhaps? I have some influence around town. Haven't I seen some articles by your Miss Morton?"

Here it was! Here was the real reason the sonofabitch was here, Quist thought. He struggled to keep his face from showing what he felt.

"Lydia is first-rate at that kind of interview feature," Quist said, his voice remarkably steady. "But I have the feeling this is a man's job. A woman writing about a man —this particular man at this particular time—would strike a sour note, I think. I might undertake it myself, or my associate, Dan Garvey, who was a professional football player and is a sports enthusiast. Either one of us would come closer, I think, to giving it the right color."

Gottfried's smile was almost a giveaway. It suggested admiration for the way Quist had handled a touchy moment. "I leave it to you, Mr. Quist," he said. "I'll make it clear to Dave Lewis he must leave it to you."

Maybe he had gotten the message Quist had meant to convey. Maybe he thought Quist was telling him he was backing away, not going to make an outcry about Lydia's absence, playing the game the way they wanted him to play it.

"I need help from you, directly or indirectly," Quist said.

"What help?"

"This is no time to talk to Mark. He's not rational. He couldn't be expected to be. But we need facts about him— his boyhood, his school and college athletics, his background. It occurs to me that Beatrice Lorimer, his aunt, might be a prime source. Could you or Mr. Lewis assure her that it's to Mark's interest for her to talk to me or to Dan Garvey freely?"

The smile was wider. "I should think that might be quite simple, Mr. Quist. May I say that my admiration for your competence has increased since meeting you?"

They had both told each other something, or had they?

"Glad you came in," Quist said.

"I'll leave word at my office you're to be put through to me any time you choose to call," Gottfried said. "In case you need me."

"I appreciate the courtesy," Quist said.

He stood and shook hands. Then he watched Gottfried walk out of the office. He bent down and pounded on his desk with both fists. The bastard knew where Lydia was and what had happened to her.

Garvey and Connie Talbot came into the room and Garvey's arm went round Quist's shoulder.

"Easy," he said.

Quist turned, his face working. "You heard him? He was testing me; trying to see how I would react to a mention of Lydia!"

"If that's the way it was, you played it just fine," Garvey said. "You as good as told him you weren't going to make an outcry; you were going to play it the way they want you to. Which, of course, you have no intention of doing. But, Julian, it's just possible that Max Gottfried doesn't know anything about Lydia's disappearance; that he was here for the exact reasons he gave you."

Quist shook his head. "I could feel it, hot and cold, up and down my spine. He knows! If you'd been on the receiving end of those gimlet eyes, you'd know, too."

"Well, you solved one problem brilliantly," Garvey said. "You got yourself out of this office without having to wear a disguise. You can go back to the Stillwell place to see Beatrice Lorimer with Gottfried's okay."

"What can I do, boss?" Connie asked.

"You can make an appointment with Dr. Milton Frankel," Garvey said, "and get over there and lay bare your neurotic subconscious—or anything else you care to lay bare."

"Louse!" Connie said.

117

chapter 3

Quist drove his car up the East River Drive toward the Triborough Bridge, his hands gripping the wheel tighter than normal. He had phoned Beatrice Lorimer and she had agreed to see him. He would arrive there about cocktail time. "We're not socializing, but of course you're welcome," she'd told Quist. "Max Gottfried called me." Quist had also called Kreevich. The detective told him they had come up with nothing very helpful in Westchester.

"Checking out alibis, just to be certain," Kreevich said. "So far everybody seems to have been where they ought to have been, including the gay Mr. Bayne and Miss Miriam Talbot. The lady spent the night at Bayne's and went back to New York the next afternoon, long after Jadwin was shot. Your friend Garvey's theory about 'muscle' is the answer, if there is a connection between the two crimes."

"You doubt it?" Quist asked.

"I think it's likely, but I need to prove it. No word from

Miss Morton?"

Quist told him there was none, and about Gottfried's visit. "I think it was a fishing expedition; trying to find out how I was reacting to Lydia's disappearance. I tried to let him think I was sitting tight."

"And aren't you?" Kreevich's voice was sharp.

"Would you in my place?"

"I'd consider the risks."

Quist's voice shook. "Does it occur to you that Lydia has almost no chance at all, Kreevich? She may be dead now; she almost certainly will be dead later. My army is going after this in its own way."

"Your army?"

"The people I'd trust with my life and Lydia's."

Kreevich hesitated. "Stay in touch with me," he said. "If there's anything from the police on Miss Morton—crime or accident—I'll know at once."

Quist sounded far away, even to himself. "If Lydia is dead, give me a little time, Kreevich."

"Time for what?"

"To wipe out the whole miserable crew of them."

"Quist—!"

Quist had hung up. He had gone to the locked drawer of a desk in his living room and taken out a handgun, a .38 police special. He had a license for it.

There was a still, deserted feeling about the Stillwell house when Quist drove up the bluestone drive to the front door. There was no one visible on the grounds, no one down in the pool area, no cars parked at the front.

Before he reached the front door, it was opened by Shallert, the houseman.

"Mrs. Lorimer is expecting you, Mr. Quist."

Quist followed him, wondering what Shallert might know, ever-present in this household. He had been questioned, of course, by Sims, and Jadwin, and probably Kreevich. Had he told everything he knew about the night of Caroline's murder? Could he possibly know what had taken Caroline down to the scene of her death?

Beatrice Lorimer came from a desk, where she'd been writing, to greet Quist. She was wearing navy blue bell-bottom pants and a pale yellow shirt, open at the throat and a little way down the front. Women her age don't usually look well in trousers, Quist thought, but Beatrice Lorimer had a magnificent figure for any age.

"You may just have saved my life, Julian," she said, holding out a hand that was warm and firm.

"How so?"

"We are almost completely deserted," she said. "Pat Grant and Jerry have both gone into the city. Mark is locked away in his study, unwilling to see or talk to anyone. I suppose that's not unnatural. I've been writing a few letters that have to be sent."

"The Lewises?" Quist asked.

"Gone. Poor Marcia. She's still in a state of uncontrolled hysteria. David finally decided she needed more care than she could get here and she's been taken to some kind of rest-home clinic somewhere on Long Island, I believe."

Beatrice crossed the room to a bar set up on a beautiful Florentine chest. "I don't drink alone on principle," she said, "which is why I've been so anxious for you to arrive, Julian. What can I make you?"

"Jack Daniels on the rocks, please," Quist said. Marcia Lewis had never been questioned by the police for medical

120

reasons. Now she was shut away somewhere, still unavailable. If could mean nothing, or it could mean that she knew too much. It wasn't a line he could follow with Beatrice. Any interest he showed in the murder case could be passed on to the people who had taken Lydia.

Beatrice made his drink and a gin and tonic for herself and joined him on the couch next to the open French windows. "Thank God there is something to talk about beside poor Caroline," she said. "Max Gottfried tells me your firm will be handling Mark's publicity in his new job."

"It involves more than publicity," Quist said. "Our job is to build the proper public image of Mark. It involves all there is to know about Mark that can be used to his advantage, as well as being aware of anything that might hurt him. We don't want anything unexpected popping out of the woodwork."

Beatrice sipped her drink. Quist was oddly reminded of a statement once made by an old actor. "No matter what a man and a woman are talking about on stage, the subject is always sex." This woman, sophisticated, beautifully turned out, was aware of it every second of the time. The way she placed herself on the couch, the way her dark violet eyes watched him, the apparently inadvertent touch of his hand when she passed him his drink, were all part of a skillfully played sex game. At another time it would have amused him, intrigued him. Now his nerves were stretched tight by his anxiety for Lydia.

"I don't think I know any man with less to hide than Mark," Beatrice said. "His father left him a business but no money. Mark built that business, and others, into a large fortune. No one has ever questioned his business integrity. I don't think he has hurt people along the way. He has always kept himself mentally alert, physically in top shape. You don't have to make him attractive. He is already that. He has been generous with charities. He has been—God help him—happily married to a lovely woman. Is it cold-blooded to suggest that what has happened to Caroline could make him an object of sympathy?"

Quist sipped his drink, his eyes averted. "It's quite realistic," he said. "I take it, then, that the rumors about Miriam Talbot are just backstairs gossip."

Quist turned, slowly, to look at her and saw that her eyes were dark with anxiety, the flirtatiousness gone from them.

"Miriam Talbot?" Beatrice said, her voice husky from sudden tension. "Miriam is Tommy Bayne's girl."

"There's always talk about important men," Quist said. "The Talbot talk is probably just mischief. But we don't want it coming out to hurt us at the wrong moment."

Ice tinkled against the glass Beatrice was holding. "What is the talk?"

Quist shrugged, as though it wasn't important. "That he's had a long-standing affair with Miriam, bed-hopping in hotels and motels, and even down the road at Bayne's cottage."

"Oh, my God," Beatrice said. "If reporters get wind of it, they'll dig and dig!"

"And find nothing—if there's nothing to find," Quist said. "Miriam is a very sexy broad. The other night she was obviously making a play for Mark. I thought it was just her way of enjoying the evening. But when I heard the talk—I wondered."

"If there's talk, it doesn't matter whether it's true or not as far as the public is concerned," Beatrice said.

"If it isn't true, it will die from lack of substance," Quist said. "I'm not interested in making moral judgments, Beatrice. I'm simply concerned with protecting my client if there's danger."

He could almost see the wheels going round in Beatrice's mind. "You and that New York detective were talking to Jerry yesterday," she said. "Did he pass this gossip along to you?"

"We asked him about it," Quist said.

"Then the detective knows! Does he think that gives him a reason to focus on Mark?"

"Focus on him?"

"He could read it as a motive for Mark's wanting to get rid of Caroline," Beatrice said. "God damn Jerry! I've been telling Mark for a long time he ought to get rid of Jerry, send him to Paris to paint, send him anywhere."

"Why?"

"You're not a blind man, Julian. You must have seen that Jerry was in love with Caroline."

Quist smiled. "So were all men who knew her—just a little. She was very special. Are you suggesting that Jerry was having a thing with her?"

"Of course not! Mark was the only man she cared about."

Quist put his glass down on the little table in front of him. "I only care about this so that it won't come at us suddenly, out of left field. If it's idle talk, we don't need to worry."

"It can't be true," Beatrice said.

"But you're not certain?"

"Of course I'm certain!"

"Then let's forget it," Quist said. "What I need from you is the story of Mark's beginnings—his school, his college, any athletics he did well in, his clubs—the works."

Beatrice went over to the bar and rebuilt her drink. The air was electric with her tension. "Somewhere in Mark's study is a folder full of biographical material. I tried to get it for you before you came, but the study door is locked. Mark won't answer a knock or his private phone. He's pretty thoroughly stunned by what's happened."

Quist watched her come back toward the couch, moving like a fine actress. The sexual woman was there, even under pressure.

"He *is* there," Quist said. It was a question.

She stopped halfway to him, glass in hand. "Of course he's there. He wouldn't go anywhere without letting me know. The police are still back and forth. Where would he go?"

Quist shrugged, and she got the message. Mark could be down the road at the Bayne cottage, locked in his lady love's arms. Quist had no doubt Jerry had told the truth about the relationship, and Beatrice knew it was true. She couldn't hide it, try as she would.

She came toward him again, and now she was playing the woman of charm to the hilt. "I'll try once more to get the folder for you—before you go," she said. "You don't have to go at once, do you? I don't look forward to a lonely supper."

"I'm in no particular hurry," Quist said.

She sat down beside him again, and her laugh was musical. "In a way I'm surprised," she said. "You don't make much effort to hide your own private world—you and Lydia Morton. I hate to concede another woman's special charms, but your Lydia is really something. I'd imagined she'd be waiting for you."

124

Here it was again—the gentle question. Would he admit she was missing? Would he show his hand?

He looked at her, fighting to keep it oh-so-casual. "Lydia is a combination of unbeatable ingredients," he said. "She is an independent woman, a top researcher and writer, drawing a salary that matches any man's in the field—and not because I love her. That satisfies women's lib shouters. She's also aware that sexual glamor is woman's most unique gift, and she uses it with skill, and tenderness, and love, and not as a weapon." He experimented with a small laugh. "I would do anything in the world for her, commit any crime for her, rob the Bank of England for her, if necessary." He didn't add that he would even let a murderer go free to guarantee her safety.

"I envy her," Beatrice said, her long eyelashes lowered.

"Why?" Quist said. "The first time I laid eyes on you I said to myself that here was another gal who, like Lydia, knew how to be all the things that make a total female."

"How very nice of you, Julian." She almost purred.

"Do you mind if I'm curious about you?" he asked.

"I'm delighted."

" 'Aunt Beatrice' doesn't fit you."

"Thank God, and nobody would dare call me that!"

"Somehow your living here with Mark and Caroline doesn't fit my concept of you; just sitting here wasting away what should be the most exciting time of your life. You should be up to your neck in some kind of public activity, and up to your neck in men." He laughed again. "Of course I may be misjudging you on the second point. You would be charmingly discreet about your love life."

She looked very pleased. "I am useful to Mark," she said.

"As a second hostess?"

She seemed to hesitate. "Mark's father was my brother," she said. "But I was the youngest of eight children. I'm actually only four years older than Mark."

"I might have thought younger except for the 'aunt' thing," Quist said.

"You're making my afternoon," Beatrice said. She reached out and touched his hand. "I worked in my father's office when I was only sixteen. I developed a very good head for figures. I was a vice-president of the Stillwell Company when Mark took over. He trusted my judgment on business matters. He still does. So you see, Julian, I'm not just sitting here wasting away. I'm here because most of Mark's important decisions are made here. He depends on me."

It was as if a small but critical piece of the puzzle had fallen suddenly into place. Quist realized he'd been fretting over certain contradictions in Mark Stillwell. The young financial genius, working round the clock, who yet had time for his daily workouts at the Athletic Club and for what was obviously a time-consuming affair with Miriam Talbot. The man with great power who could use that power meanly against his brother, and apparently with generosity toward Beatrice. Maybe it all came together with this hint from Beatrice. A phony businessman, a phony husband, a put-together power symbol; a puppet in the financial world with this complex woman pulling the strings. Quist remembered the little scene on the terrace when he and Kreevich had arrived there yesterday; Beatrice and David Lewis sitting together. They were the real brains of the combine, if he was right. Mark was a dummy figure. Mark could be the really weak link in the chain of power. They would protect him at any cost from his indiscretions, because he was a front they manipulated and used.

Beatrice had let her foot slip just a little, Quist thought. Her power drive and her sex drive had gotten tangled together for a moment. She had wanted to build herself up for this attractive man who sat next to her on the couch, and she had told him a little more than she had intended. She must have guessed what he was thinking and she tried to undo the damage.

"Don't misunderstand, Julian," she said. "I'm not any sort of financial wizard, but Mark likes to talk over his ideas and I make a good sounding board for them. We were trained by my brother—his father—to think alike."

Don't let her worry about it too much, Quist thought. In a flirtatious moment she might have given him the only weapon he had.

"It's hard for me to think of you in anything but woman terms," he said, smiling. "Is it being too curious to ask about a Mr. Lorimer?"

She sipped her drink. "When you are learning to walk, you inevitably fall down and skin your knees," she said. "Robert Lorimer was a young lawyer working for my father. I had a crush on him as an adolescent. Overnight I—I became a woman and I was set on fire when he touched me. We skipped off to Greenwich and got married, a popular sport in those days. It wasn't very long before my fires went out, and Robert wasn't much good for anything else. My father was quite happy to help me untie the knot."

"And you never tried again?"

Her eyes invited him. "Marriage, as an institution, never again seemed a necessary part of pleasure to me. I suspect you understand that, Julian, or you and Miss Morton would be married."

"How perceptive of you," he said. "But to get back to why I'm here, Beatrice. To build a true picture of Mark, remember? You'll get me the biographical folder?"

"As soon as Mark comes out of seclusion," she said.

"You care to talk at all about David Lewis? Because he's the real power behind this Sports Complex, of course."

Something in Beatrice's manner changed. She seemed to withdraw, grow cautious. "An interesting man," she said. "He really belongs to another generation. He started out as a messenger boy on the Stock Exchange, not a dime to his name."

"The Horatio Alger legend?" Quist suggested.

She nodded. "Power only comes to people who dream of power day and night. You only build great wealth from scratch if it's all you want. That's David. Today he controls more in this industrial society than you would believe. He influences business, he influences government. His intricate maneuverings make him an altogether fascinating character."

"To a business woman like yourself?"

"To any kind of woman," Beatrice said. " 'Ask and ye shall receive.' That kind of man is fascinating to any woman."

"Is he sexually attractive?"

Beatrice's eyes narrowed. "I don't quite know how to answer that—for you, Julian. You see, when you mature a little—which is a delicate way of saying 'at my age'—you aren't sexually attracted by muscles, or profiles, or erotic fantasies. Giving yourself to a man is like—like adding an ingredient to a drink." She held up her glass. "Gin alone is

128

a little raw, a little harsh. Add tonic to it and it becomes a delightful drink. Tonic alone is nothing. If you think mixing the ingredients will produce something delightful, then you have sexual excitement." She looked at Quist directly. "Mixing what is me with you suggests a pleasurable result; a kind of carefree fun, a kind of no-strings-attached gaiety that is rare. The idea is sexually exciting. Mixing what is me with David Lewis would promise something quite different—access to special power, access to all the world's luxuries, a chance to move important chess pieces on the world's game board. I would guess that makes David attractive to many women." She smiled. "A sophisticated woman knows that withholding sex often gets her more than giving. I wanted something for Mark from David. He may have been exciting while I played for that, but now that Mark has it, David seems to have lost his attraction."

"His wife puzzled me a little," Quist said. "A man who can buy anything he wants might be expected to have a very glamorous woman. Mrs. Lewis is almost mousy."

"A long-time marriage," Beatrice said. "You know, some men like to break wild horses. Some like to whip animals whose spirits are broken."

Quist's eyebrows rose. "You mean Lewis beats his wife?"

Beatrice laughed. "Only figuratively, I hope. As a matter of fact I was surprised and touched by his concern for her here. It seems there are, at least, the remnants of a very real love for her." She put down her glass and stood up. "I'll see if I can persuade Mark to give me that folder." She hesitated. "We have been playing a very pleasant game here, Julian, which I know doesn't interest you at the moment beyond the talking stage. But if ever you tire of Miss Morton, or she of you, you might be surprised at the kind of drink we could mix."

It was after eight o'clock, but still daylight, when Quist opened the door of his apartment and went in. For a brief instant his heart jammed against his ribs. There was someone in the kitchenette. Lydia?

Connie Paramalee appeared in the kitchenette doorway. Her eyes narrowed behind the tinted granny glasses. She sensed what he had hoped for a moment.

"Sorry it's only me," she said.

She had a key to his apartment which he couldn't remember her ever having used before. She looked particularly attractive in a plain black dress with a schoolgirl's white collar and cuffs—and a nice expanse of leg.

"There were messages—and I thought if you stopped here, there should be someting for you to eat and drink. Have you eaten anything all day?"

"What messages?"

"Lieutenant Kreevich has nothing to report to you. Will you call Max Gottfried at your convenience. I have his home phone. Dan thinks he's on the trail of something—but he didn't say what. Bobby is taking Miriam Talbot to the circus."

"I suspect she doesn't need instruction on the trapeze," Quist said. He sat down because he felt his legs wouldn't hold out much longer. Nothing was hard to bear. "Oh, God, Connie, this thing is eating away at my gut like acid."

"I know. No luck on your end?"

"I had a pass made at me by a beautiful lady, and I discovered that Mark Stillwell is made of cardboard," Quist said. He explained. "So he may be the weak spot we can

130

use—when we can use anything."

"Drink? Coffee?" Connie asked.

"Some bourbon in some coffee," he said. He closed his eyes as Connie went out to the kitchenette. He couldn't take it this way! He had to act to find Lydia. He couldn't just pull away and pray. But act in a vacuum? You couldn't just flail around in space. He needed leverage against someone just as important to the killer as Lydia was to him.

Connie came back from the kitchenette, stopping at the bar to lace his coffee with bourbon.

"I saw Dr. Frankel," she said casually.

"Oh?"

"My doctor knows him, so I was able to arrange for an emergency appointment. My doctor has been making passes at me for so long he's ready to do almost anything to make me sufficiently grateful," Connie said. "I am, he told Dr. Frankel, badly disturbed. It would be a professional favor—et cetera, et cetera, et cetera."

"Did you tell your doctor why you wanted to see Frankel?"

"I told him," Connie said, her face expressionless, "that I wanted to rob the doctor's safe. Naturally he didn't believe me, which is why I told him the truth. But he hopes I will become his slave."

"So what happened?"

"So Dr. Frankel received me with courtesy. I lay down on his couch, showing as much leg as I could without seeming to be intentionally provocative. He asked me politely what my problem was. I told him."

Quist gave her a tired smile. "And what is your problem?"

"None of your business," Connie said. "I thought I might get some useful advice as long as I was there. The point is —there are no files, no safe in either the waiting room or the consulting room. Patients are not encouraged to look for anything in case the good doctor has to go to the john in the middle of a session. I suspect there is a private office, or study, off the consulting room, but I had no chance to look there."

"I hope you got some good advice."

"It better be good—for fifty bucks," Connie said. "What do you bet that Mrs. Lewis is the Herr Doktor's patient?"

"It might be a very good bet," Quist said. "If we can find out where they've taken her, she just might be a help." He twisted in his chair. "Connie, if you were Lydia, what would you want me to do?"

Connie's eyes were shaded by the tinted glasses. "I'd expect you to work a miracle," she said.

"What kind of miracle?"

"I wouldn't worry about that. I'd just count on you."

"And I'm just sitting here!"

"That could be the miracle," Connie said. "It may take more guts to do nothing than to charge down Fifth Avenue, like Errol Flynn, brandishing a sword."

The telephone rang and Quist nodded to Connie to answer it. He saw her face tighten, then she held the phone out to him. "It's not about Lydia," she said, "but it is Lieutenant Kreevich."

Kreevich had that crisp, hard sound. "One-two punch," he said. "Your man Garvey—"

"What about him?"

"He's in Bellevue Hospital," Kreevich said. "Somebody

beat the hell out of him. Listed as critical. He can't tell us anything."

"Who did it? Where did it happen?"

"He was found in an alley between houses on West Tenth Street," Kreevich said. "Building superintendent carrying out some garbage fell over him. Nobody saw or heard anything. Garvey put up a hell of a fight, from the way he looks. He got a highly professional beating. You know what he was doing in that part of town?"

"Following a lead is the message I got," Quist said. "But not what lead."

"Maybe you better get down here to the hospital," Kreevich said. "I'll wait for you."

Part Three

chapter 1

Quist's face looked as if it had been carved out of some kind of pale rock as he stood looking down at the hospital bed where Dan Garvey lay, his head swathed in bandages, his eyes closed. Garvey's breathing had a shallow sound to it.

Connie, who had made a wild taxi ride downtown with Quist, had turned away toward the shaded window. Her professional cool had deserted her and she was crying softly.

Lieutenant Kreevich and a doctor in a green surgical suit stood across the bed from Quist.

"Touch-and-go is the best I can give you, Mr. Quist," the doctor said. He spoke in a low voice as if he didn't want Garvey to hear. It was clear Garvey couldn't have heard the angel Gabriel's horn if it had sounded. "He was terribly beaten around the head—jaw broken, and I'm guessing a skull fracture or fractures. X-rays will tell for sure. A few body bruises that you might expect after a fight, but nothing there of any consequence."

"The wounds suggest a leaded billy or sock—iron pipe covered with something," Kreevich said. "Skin scarcely broken, but the damage—well, violent force used."

"X-rays will be along presently," the doctor said. "We'll know then about surgery—if he can take it."

Quist's lips moved without any sound emerging. He was swearing silently, methodically.

"He hasn't said anything, hasn't talked," Kreevich said. "No telling when he will or can."

"I wouldn't hold my breath," the doctor said.

Quist turned away. "Anything he needs, Doctor. Anything at all."

"A little prayer is the only thing I can suggest," the doctor said.

Down the corridor from Garvey's room was a little alcove with chairs, a place where people waited. Quist thought he had seen the scene played a hundred times— friends or relatives waiting, the doctor coming down the corridor toward them with news that would change their entire lives.

"I need help," Kreevich said.

"God, don't we all!" Quist said.

"You said on the phone Garvey was following a lead?"

"We're all searching for some clue that will help us find Lydia," Quist said. He glanced at Connie.

"He phoned Mr. Quist's apartment early in the evening," Connie said. "I was there—to take messages if they came. Dan just said 'I may be onto something—but don't get your hopes up. I'll call when I can.' That was that."

"Where it happened is an alley running between buildings

about halfway down the block on Tenth Street between Fifth and Sixth," Kreevich said. "The alley goes straight through the block to Eleventh Street, between some fenced-in garden patches behind the houses that face on both streets. Building superintendent takes care of three or four houses. He was collecting trash to put out for the Sanitation truck in the morning. Literally stumbled over Garvey near the Tenth Street mouth of the alley. It was dark."

Quist shook his head. "I have no idea what Dan could have been doing in that part of town. Does he have friends down there, Connie?"

"Dan's private life is very private," Connie said.

Kreevich scowled at an unlit cigarette in his fingers. "How loud does the message have to be shouted at you?" he asked Quist. "If you care anything about the safety of your girl, shouldn't you back off completely? See what it got your friend."

Quist took hold of the detective's arm and saw him wince from the force of the grip. "Lydia has no chance if we just sit back and wait for the thing to unfold. They can't let her go. She could talk. My one hope is that they've kept her alive in case they need to use her."

"How?"

"A direct message to me—a phone call. Something to convince me she's alive and I'd better do what they say. After that—!" Quist let go Kreevich's arm and turned away.

"They're watching you, they were obviously watching Garvey. They're a step ahead of you, no matter which way you turn. Because you don't know who's watching."

"What do you suggest?"

"I wish I could tell you something practical, something

reassuring. I can't."

"Maybe I can give you something practical," Quist said. "Find Mrs. Lewis. She's been taken away to some kind of rest home on Long Island—somewhere none of us can talk to her. I'm betting she's Frankel's patient. If so, he can tell you where she is. Concentrate a little on Beatrice Lorimer and Patrick Grant. I think Mark Stillwell is a dummy figure, with Beatrice the real brains and power in that setup. I'm betting Marcia Lewis saw something that none of them, the Stillwell crowd or the Lewis crowd, can afford to have revealed. The one chance Lydia has, Kreevich, is for somebody to spill the whole beans before they've done her in. Only if we can find out everything in time—that's her one chance. So that what she can tell us is no longer dangerous, because we already know it. Marcia Lewis could be our best hope."

Kreevich nodded slowly. "I'll find Mrs. Lewis," he said.

"It's too late for it to be tomorrow or the next day!" Quist almost shouted. "If Dan was onto something—"

"I will also do my best to protect Garvey," Kreevich said.

"Protect him! For Christ sake, he's almost dead now!"

"He was beaten up because he found out something—don't you think?" Kreevich said. "He was left for dead in that alley. But he isn't dead—not yet. The news story has gone out before I could stop it—that he isn't dead. Once he opens his baby blue eyes and speaks, someone has had it. So his room, this whole floor, is going to be covered like a tent."

"It's like a snowball, growing bigger and bigger!" Connie said.

Kreevich lit his cigarette. "That's the way it goes in any

140

kind of criminal conspiracy to hide the truth. It's like a Watergate. More and more people become involved, more and more crimes are committed to hide an initial truth. If Jadwin had been able to arrest Caroline Stillwell's murderer that first night, your Miss Morton would have been untouched, Garvey and you would be living your normal lives. Take a look at it. Mrs. Stillwell saw something on the grounds of her house and ran out to do something about what she saw. She was killed and angrily cut up. Not a planned murder. Now let's guess. Mrs. Lewis saw something and went blubbering to her husband and perhaps the others about it. It involved someone important to them. Caroline Stillwell couldn't be helped, so let's hide it so 'our mountain' doesn't fall down. The Fates seem to play on their side. Johnny Tiptoe wanders onto the grounds and looks like the perfect fall guy. They hear his story, and somebody sneaks down to the gardener's tool shed, gets some gasoline, and fills the tank in Tiptoe's jalopy to discredit him, make it tighter, not knowing that your Mr. Hilliard had already checked it out empty. Jadwin starts looking their way. He has to be stopped. You, Quist, pick up the ball and you have to be stopped before you can get to Mrs. Lewis and she blows the whole ball game. The best way to stop you is to immobilize you through Lydia Morton. But your man Garvey blunders on and comes across the truth, or part of it. He has to die. So you see, they can't stop their violence now. It has to go on and on." He looked calmly at Quist and Connie Parmalee. "I know how you feel. I know the fury that's cooking in you. I know it's no use my telling you to lay off, back away, leave it to us. You'll explode from it if you just sit still and do nothing. But I urge you—you and all your people, Quist—not to forget Caroline Stillwell's mutilated body or Garvey's smashed skull for a single moment. The same kind of thing is waiting round the corner for all of you!"

Connie's eyes were unblinking behind her tinted glasses. "Dan may have made some phone calls, maybe some notes, in his office," she said. "Would it help if I checked with his secretary, went to his office to have a look?"

"It might help a lot," Kreevich said. "But please watch your step, Miss Parmalee."

"I'll go with her," Quist said. Where else was there for him to go?

Quist and Connie rode uptown in a taxi to the office. They sat close together, her hand locked in his. They were hanging onto each other for mutual survival. Quist found himself involved with slightly mad fantasies. An eye for an eye. He would go out to Westchester, grab off Mark Stillwell and break every bone in his body, one by one, until he was ready to talk. Or what about the sexy Miss Talbot? Would Mark want her back as badly as he wanted Lydia? He thought, bitterly, not. Mark would always come first with Mark. He would seduce Beatrice Lorimer into going off on a sex date with him, and then hang her up by her fingernails until she would tell what she knew. He would go to Dr. Frankel's fancy Park Avenue offices and tear them to pieces until he found proof that Marcia Lewis was the doctor's patient, and force Frankel to tell where she was being hidden.

"You're hurting my hand, Julian," Connie said.

He looked down and saw that his hand was dead-white from pressure.

"My dear Connie, I'm sorry. I—I think I want to kill somebody."

The night man in the lobby of the office building knew them well. They often came in after hours and signed in on his chart.

"Busy night," he said. "There's others upstairs tonight."

"Oh?" Quist said.

The man waved at his chart. "Mr. Hilliard and Miss Chard," he said.

They went up in the elevator, self-service at this time of night. Quist opened the office door with his key. Lights were on brightly in the reception room, and they heard Gloria Chard's musical laughter coming from down the hall. Quist called out.

Gloria and Bobby Hilliard appeared together. Gloria was wearing an eye-catching dark blue dinner dress that Quist knew had been designed by Marilyn Martin. It was cut to reveal a considerable amount of bare shoulders and a delightful cleavage.

"You've heard about Dan?" Bobby asked, his boyish face creased with anxiety.

"We've just come from the hospital," Quist said.

"How bad is it?" Gloria asked. It was rumored in the office that she and Garvey spent a good deal of their spare time together.

"Bad," Quist said.

"I wanted to go down to Bellevue myself," Gloria said, "but both Bobby and I felt we should see you. We couldn't find you at home and we each came here, from our separate adventures—or nonadventures—on the chance you'd check in. Can anyone do anything for Dan?"

"The doctor suggested prayer."

"Oh, God," Gloria said. "Poor Dan! Do they know how it happened?"

"Not yet."

Connie had gone off down the hall toward Garvey's office.

"Neither Bobby or I had any success," Gloria said. "Bobby came closest."

"I took Miriam Talbot to the circus," Bobby said.

"Rather an adolescent choice of pleasures for a sexy dame," Quist said.

"Oh, it was her choice," Bobby said. "I hate the circus. Can't bear to watch those people on the high wires and trapezes. Miriam seemed to get a big kick out of it, almost as if she hoped someone would fall!"

"Would she talk at all—about Mark?"

"I tried, never being very direct," Bobby said. "I—I had the feeling she was laughing at me, as though she knew perfectly well why I'd asked her out. As though that's why she'd accepted, to find out what I wanted. I had to play it very cagey."

"And?"

"And then, as we were leaving the forum and I was wondering what to suggest next, she suggested. Why didn't I come back to her place? She actually laughed and said she'd like to get into something comfortable. The cliché of all time, and she knew it.

"I was trying to get a taxi when a kid came along selling morning papers. That early edition had Dan on the front page. 'FORMER FOOTBALL STAR CRITICALLY HURT IN MUGGING.' There was an old picture of Dan from his football days. Miriam seemed jarred by it. She suddenly, she told me, had a bad migraine headache. If I'd forgive her, she'd hurry home alone. She left me standing at the curb with my mouth hanging open, it was that fast."

"So no results?"

"None—except that she never had any doubts about what I really wanted from her. And was laughing at me!"

"I didn't do as well as Bobby," Gloria said. "I went to see Patrick Grant at the offices of Stillwell Enterprises this afternoon. All on the up and up—part of the Sports Complex promotion. He had me taken into his private office past other people who were ahead of me." Gloria smiled. "I had on one of Rudi Gernreich's best. I looked wonderful, if you don't mind my saying so. I batted my eyelashes at him and wriggled my torso a little. I could see the lights going on behind his eyes. He explained, regretfully, that he couldn't give me time then. He was swamped with things he had to do for Mark, who because of the tragedy was, quite naturally, salted away somewhere. However—and those lights got very bright—he'd just love to take me out on the town tonight. He couldn't take me to dinner, but he'd buy me a champagne supper at any place I chose. We could talk about the Sports Complex—and anything else that seemed like fun to talk about—over caviar. He'd pick me up at my apartment at nine o'clock. He wrote down the address and the telephone number. He gave my arm a suggestive little squeeze as we parted—and that was that! He never showed up, he never phoned. The s.o.b. stood me up. First time in my life!"

"Sounds as though we'd scared them off," Quist said, frowning. "Too much action in too many sectors."

"What do you suppose Dan got onto?" Bobby Hilliard asked. "I'd swear the news really jolted my Miss Talbot."

Connie called to them from Garvey's office down the hall. Quist went to join her, followed by Bobby and Gloria. Garvey's office was very specially his own, differing from the modern art and color schemes of the rest of the place.

The paneled walls were covered with photographs of people prominent in the world of sports, all autographed to Garvey, and group pictures of teams on which he played in school, college, and later in pro football.

Connie was standing at Garvey's desk, frowning down at a scratch pad she was holding. She glanced at Quist. "Nothing much here, boss," she said. "I got Dan's secretary at home. She says there was nothing outside regular routines for Dan. He was out from lunchtime on. Called a couple of times to see if there was any word from you. I don't find anything on his appointment pad or this doodling pad—except this." She handed the pad to Quist.

Garvey was a notorious doodler. There were geometrical designs, and funny faces, and words spelled out in rigid Gothic letters. Two of the words were a man's name—Ed Vickers.

"He starts with that pad clean every morning," Connie said. "Whatever's there is today's accumulation."

"No girls with bulging bosoms," Quist muttered. "The name Ed Vickers mean anything to you?"

Connie nodded. "It rang some kind of a bell with me," she said. She motioned to one of the group pictures on the wall. "His college football team."

Quist went to look at the picture. It was a typical group-team thing—one row of players sitting on the ground, a second row sitting behind them on a bench, a third row standing. Underneath the photograph Garvey had written: UNDEFEATED STATE 1963. The team captain, a huge young blond, sat in the center of the second row holding a football. Next to him was Garvey, looking incredibly boyish. All the names were printed underneath the caption. The team captain, holding the ball, was Ed Vickers.

Quist turned away. "Old college friend called him. He scribbled the name on his pad."

"In Gothic," Connie said absently. She was turning the pages of a Manhattan telephone directory. She bent down, running a finger down a column of names. Then, finger holding her place, she looked up at Quist, and her eyes behind the tinted lenses were wide. "Edward Vickers has a listing in Manhattan."

"So what's special about that?" Quist said. He wasn't interested in Garvey's old college chum.

"It's his address that's interesting," Connie said. "He lives on West Eleventh Street. It has to be quite close to where Dan was found."

Quist stood straight and still, staring at her.

"You want me to call him and see if Dan connected with him earlier?" Connie asked.

"I think not," Quist said. "I think I'll make an unannounced call on Mr. Vickers."

Twenty-six West Eleventh Street was a remodeled brownstone house, cut up into small apartments. It actually adjoined the alley in which Dan Garvey had been found.

Quist checked the vestibule and found the name VICKERS over the bell for the second floor rear apartment. Quist hesitated. Connie had begged him not to come alone, but he had sent her to his apartment to wait. There might be some attempt at contact by whoever had Lydia. The Vickers lead might be a total coincidence, he told her, and somehow didn't believe it for an instant. Dan had been found, almost dead, in the dark alley right next to this house. There was the chance, of course, that Vickers was a friend, a perfectly good, honest friend. Dan could have

147

thought of him, scribbled his name on the desk pad, called him and come down here for help or information of some sort. He could have been attacked before he got to Vickers or after he left him. But if Dan had called Vickers, or gotten to him, Vickers would know what Dan was after.

Quist drew a deep breath and pressed the buzzer for 2R. A moment later a voice came over the speaker system.

"Yeah?"

Quist spoke into the house phone. "Mr. Vickers? I'm a friend of Dan Garvey's. Can you spare me a minute?"

"Dan Garvey!" The voice was cheerful. "How do you like that? Sure. Come on up."

The door lock clicked, and Quist let himself in.

It was a nicely kept house. There was a table for mail or messages, carefully dusted. The hall and stair carpeting looked as if it had been vacuumed not too long ago. Quist knew the type of building. These would be two-room apartments, renting for about three hundred, three hundred and fifty dollars a month.

Quist started the climb to the second floor, but before he was halfway up, a giant figure of a man appeared at the head of the stairs. He must have been six feet nine or ten inches tall, and weighing at least two hundred and fifty pounds, all muscle. He had a shaggy head of blond hair and a bright, white smile. He was wearing a short-sleeved sports shirt that revealed awesome forearms. When Quist reached him, he felt his hand taken in a bone-crushing grip.

"Friend of Dan's?" Vickers said. "How is the old sonofabitch?"

"My name is Julian Quist. Dan works for me."

"Come on in, Julian. It's never too late for a drink, in my book. Come in, come in."

148

Quist guessed that the giant Vickers rented this apartment furnished, or borrowed it from a lady friend. The furniture all looked too fragile for him.

"What'll it be?" Vickers asked, heading for a side table where some liquor bottles rested. "I was just going to have a nightcap all by my lonesome." It sounded almost coy coming from this giant.

"Bourbon, if you've got it," Quist said. "Rocks, if you've got ice."

"Coming up," Vickers said. "I'm glad to see you, Julian boy, but you've got me guessing." His hand seemed to cover the whole glass when he handed it to Quist.

Quist felt an unexplained tension rising in him. There was nothing hostile or suspicious about Vickers. He decided to play it straight.

"Dan's had a bad thing happen," he said. "Earlier tonight he was found, unconscious, in the alley that runs between your house and the next. He's in Bellevue hospital, listed critical."

"For Christ sake!" Vickers said. "Right next door?"

"He was found by the building superintendent."

"He's going to make it, though, isn't he?"

"We hope. He hasn't regained consciousness. There's a chance he never will."

Vickers didn't show relief or concern. Just shock. "This goddamned city is full of muggers," he said.

"We've been trying to find out what brought Dan down to this part of town," Quist said. "Your name was written on his desk pad."

"My name? How do you like that?"

"He has a picture of your college football team on his office wall. I recognized you in it."

"That was a pretty great team," Vickers said. "We took everyone that last year. Had a Bowl bid and took that one, too. Dan was the best running back I ever saw; wizard in an open field."

"I figured, with your name on his pad, Dan might have called you, perhaps come down here to see you. Being found right next to you downstairs—"

Vickers' big face looked like a puzzled child's. "I haven't seen or heard from Dan in seven—eight years," he said. "I mean, we went different ways. He made it in big-time football. I was too slow." He grinned. "They got guys my size in the pros who can run the hundred in ten flat. We were close in school, but we went separate ways, like I said. My name on his pad! How do you like that."

"He didn't phone you?"

"No. Boy, I'd have been glad to see him. Maybe he decided to surprise me by dropping in and got mugged before he made it."

"It must have been that way," Quist said. He hadn't touched the drink Vickers had brought him. The unexplained feeling of tension was suddenly unbearable. Vickers couldn't have appeared more natural, more innocent, more properly concerned. And yet—

It suddenly came clear to Quist what was distressing him. They weren't alone in the apartment. There was someone else in the bedroom, or the kitchenette, or the bathroom. The lady whose apartment this was, he thought. It was the faint aroma of perfume that had him on edge.

"Look, I'm sorry," he said. "I didn't interrupt something, did I—coming up now?"

"Hell, no," Vickers said. "Drink up, pal. Is there anything I can do for Dan?"

"What you can do," Quist said, forcing a smile, "is to let me use your plumbing."

"Sure, help yourself," Vickers said, undisturbed. "Just through that door next to the bedroom."

Quist put down his drink and stood up. His leg muscles ached. He went through the far door. Standing inside, he could see into the bedroom, neat and undisturbed. There was no one in the kitchenette. He opened the bathroom door, half expecting to come face to face with some ally of Vickers'. It was empty. He closed the door and stood looking at himself in the mirror over the washbasin. His eyes looked as if they were staring back at him through the burned holes in a sheet.

It came over him with a kind of blinding certainty. He knew now why his pulse had started to pound at his temples the minute he'd come into Vickers' apartment. The sense of someone else—the sense of a female presence—a perfume.

He knew now what had happened to Garvey. Garvey had come here unannounced. Garvey must have got upstairs without ringing Vickers' bell. He had probably knocked on the door, and when Vickers opened it an inch or two, Garvey had forced his way in and found the lady who'd been there.

The perfume was unmistakable. It had been made by Bellini for just one person—Lydia!

Quist looked down at the palms of his hands. They were damp with sweat. Lydia wasn't here now, but she had been here not too long ago. The Bellini magic wasn't a cloying scent that would last forever.

The right move now, Quist knew, might be the difference between life and death for Lydia. He tried to think quickly back along Dan Garvey's trail. He had been looking for David Lewis's "muscle"—or Mark Stillwell's "muscle." Somewhere, on one trail or the other, he'd come across a familiar name—the name of his old college football captain. Garvey must have known something about Vickers; they'd gone different ways, according to Vickers, but Dan must have known something about the "way" Vickers had gone.

There was that, and there was one thing more. Something, some fact which Quist didn't have, must have connected Vickers with the Lewis-Stillwell combination. Dan wouldn't have come down here tonight just to cut up touches with an old college chum. He'd expected to catch, Vickers unprepared, and he'd caught him too damned unprepared. He'd caught him with Lydia here, a prisoner.

Dan was a pretty tough guy himself, but that blond giant in the next room had been too much. Vickers had destroyed Dan, carried him down to the alley, and left him there for dead. He must be doing a little sweating of his own right now, having learned that Dan was still alive. If Dan came to and talked, Vickers was done for. Vickers' next move, after he'd handled Dan, was to get Lydia away from here. Dan might have left a trail. That had to mean that either there was someone who could take over from Vickers as Lydia's jailer, or Lydia was floating among the grapefruit rinds and other garbage in the North River.

There was a knock on the bathroom door. "You okay, pal?" Vickers called out.

"Fine," Quist said. "Be out in a second."

He straightened up, fighting for composure. Then he turned and flushed the unused toilet. He stepped out of the bathroom and into the sitting room. Vickers was refreshing

152

his drink. There was one change. Vickers had put on a seersucker jacket over his sports shirt. He was planning to go somewhere, Quist thought, when his guest was gone. He didn't look at Quist as he spoke, very casually.

"You say Dan's at Bellevue?" he asked.

"Yes. Intensive care unit at the moment."

"I'd like to be able to ask for him," Vickers said. "Do something for him when he comes around."

"If he comes around," Quist said.

Vickers turned. He had pasted on his wide, white smile. "Dan's a tough cookie. He'll make it. He has to make it."

"I hope," Quist said.

"I'd make a bet," Vickers said. He gulped down his drink.

Quist measured him, knowing that his chances of over-powering this man and choking the truth out of him were slim. The best chance for Lydia, if there was a chance, was to get out of here alive and get help. He was certain Vick-ers would try to get to Dan and silence him permanently before he could talk. Kreevich, warned, would be ready for him.

"Thanks for the drink," Quist said. "You can understand how I thought you might explain what had happened to Dan, might help to establish the time it happened. If it was after he visited with you, we could just about be certain it happened as he walked out of this building. They dragged him into the alley and beat him up."

"Only he never did get here," Vickers said. "I'd appre-ciate it if you'd let me know how he does. My number's in the phone book."

"I know. That's how I got your address."

"I'm surprised you didn't phone me."

Quist gambled. "I did," he said, "but you must have been out."

Out disposing of Lydia!

"That's right," Vickers said. "I went down to a delicatessen on Sixth Avenue for a few minutes. Well, tell Dan I know about him and I'm concerned for him."

"I'll do that," Quist said. "Thanks again."

"Sorry I couldn't help," Vickers said.

It was all so casual, all so polite, and they were both thinking of murder, Quist thought. They shook hands.

Quist went out and down the carpeted stairway, the small hairs prickling on the back of his neck. When he reached the ground floor, he turned and looked back up. Vickers was smiling down at him from the second-floor landing. He waved a monstrous hand at him.

Quist went out the front door and moved quickly out into the center of the street. Vickers might just have friends waiting near the mouth of that alley, although Quist had the feeling that Ed Vickers worked alone.

He hurried toward Sixth Avenue, looking for a pay phone. At last he found one on a street corner, dialed the hospital, and asked for Kreevich. He was told the Lieutenant wasn't there.

"Then put me on to whoever's in charge of the police guard there! It's urgent."

Presently a calm voice came on. "Sergeant Winston here."

"This is Julian Quist. I was there earlier with Lieutenant Kreevich."

"I know, Mr. Quist."

"I think I know who beat up my friend Garvey. He's a man named Ed Vickers. I think he may be heading for the

154

hospital to make sure Garvey doesn't talk. There hasn't been any change?"

"No, sir. I won't take time to ask you why you think this Vickers may be our man. Can you describe him?"

"You can't miss him," Quist said. "Football player, six-nine, six-ten tall, blond, weighs two-fifty, two-sixty. He has an apartment at Twenty-six West Eleventh Street, right next to the alley where Garvey was found."

"He won't get to Garvey," the sergeant said.

"I think he'll make a damned good-sized effort," Quist said.

"He won't get to him, Mr. Quist."

"How do I reach Kreevich? There's more to this than I have time to tell you on the phone."

"You might find him at home," Winston said. "He hadn't had any sleep for about thirty-six hours. You know how to get him there?"

"I have his number. Make sure of Garvey. This guy Vickers is playing for his own life," Quist said.

"If he comes here, he's played it wrong," Winston said. "We'll have his apartment covered in a few minutes."

"I think he's already on his way," Quist said.

chapter 2

Lieutenant Kreevich had listened to a distracted man on the telephone. He knew Quist well enough to be certain he wasn't plagued by an overactive imagination. When Quist said he knew that Lydia Morton had been in Vickers' apartment, Kreevich accepted it as a fact. But how to prove it? He wasn't going to get a search warrant on the basis that Quist had "smelled" his girl in Vickers' place.

"You found an earring you can identify," Kreevich said.

"But I didn't."

"You found an earring you can identify," Kreevich said. "Meet me at my office and bring that earring. That's the only way I can get a search warrant."

"You're going to fake evidence?" Quist asked.

Kreevich sounded hurt. "You're going to bring me that earring and swear to me you found it in Vickers' apartment, friend. If you're lying to me, I can't help that, can I?"

156

"I get it," Quist said. "You think your man at the hospital can protect Garvey?"

"If he can't, nobody can."

Everything took time, precious time. Taxis were scarce, and by the time Quist hailed one and got back to his apartment on Beekman Place, a half hour was gone. Connie Parmalee was sleeping on his couch when he got there. While he searched in the dressing room on the second floor of the duplex for a small jewel case Lydia kept there, he brought Connie up to date. She reminded him that he hadn't called Max Gottfried in response to the message the lawyer had left much earlier.

"He called again about half an hour ago, boss. He says it's urgent."

Quist found the jewel case, and in it a pair of lapis earrings he'd given Lydia for her birthday a year ago. He slipped one of them in his jacket pocket. He felt whipsawed.

Connie's level stare wouldn't let him go. "It could be something about Lydia," she said.

"His first call came long ago, before—" He hesitated. Perhaps not before Garvey had found her at Vickers' place. "Get him for me, Connie."

He followed her downstairs and poured himself a cup of coffee from the ever-ready percolator while she dialed and waited.

"I have Mr. Quist, Mr. Gottfried." Connie held out the phone to him.

"I'm sorry to disturb you at this time of night, Quist," Gottfried sounded unfriendly.

"I'm in a great hurry at the moment," Quist said.

"Take time to listen," Gottfried said. "You and your firm

are to drop all activity to promote Mark Stillwell and the Sports Complex until further orders."

"Orders from who?"

"From my client, David Lewis, who is also your employer. He doesn't like the way you're going about it, Quist. He wants to talk to you before you go any further."

"What is it he doesn't like?"

"He hasn't discussed it with me," Gottfried said. "But I am to tell you this: You are to withdraw from all aspects of the situation as of now, this moment, or action will be taken against you that can't be undone at a later date."

"What kind of action?"

"I'm quoting orders to you, Quist. I don't know what Mr. Lewis has in mind. But I can tell you one thing from experience. When David Lewis threatens action of some sort, he isn't bluffing."

Quist drew a deep breath. "You can tell Lewis that you delivered his message, chum," he said. "You can also tell him that I understand exactly what he meant me to understand. You can also tell him that if he takes the action he's threatening, I will personally see to it that he's eliminated from the face of the earth."

"That's pretty wild talk, Quist."

"It is, isn't it?" Quist said. "Well, I don't bluff either, counselor. The only way you can possibly sleep well is that you don't know what the hell either Lewis or I are talking about."

Quist put down the phone and flexed his fingers, stiff from holding the instrument so tightly. "That was it," he said to Connie.

"Lydia?" she asked in a flat voice.

"As plainly as if he'd spelled it out," Quist said. "I drop

it now, this instant, or else—"

"So you drop it," Connie said.

He looked down at the wide eyes behind the tinted glasses. He took her by the shoulders and, for an instant, drew her close to him. He needed the touch of another loving human being to keep from shouting out his anguish.

"It's too late to stop," he said. "They can't let her go. She can identify Vickers even if Dan doesn't pull through to do it first. There's only one last faint hope for Lydia."

"That is?"

"Turn the heat on them and make it so hot I have a bargaining position. It may already be too late, but if it is—"

"Julian, whatever has happened, however dreadful it is, you've got your own life to live. Let Kreevich take it from here!"

"If it's happened, love, I have just one thing to live for. I'll get even in a way so spectacular it will go down in history!" He bent down and kissed her on the forehead. "Pray for us all, Connie, if you know how."

"The human mind," Kreevich said, sounding like a schoolteacher, "is like a computer, filled with a great conglomeration of facts. The difference between the mechanical brain and the human brain is that it can sort out the information you need by simply pressing a button. You don't have to dig for it."

He was sitting at his desk in his office at Headquarters. He handed Quist a roll of paper that looked like extra wide ticker tape. "We have fed everything into the computer that relates to the Stillwell case—names, data, biographies, seemingly unrelated facts. I have also fed the name of Edward Vickers into the monster, with only his name, address, telephone number and the fact that he was captain of the State football team in nineteen sixty-three. I then ask the monster two questions. Does Edward Vickers have a police record? Is there anything to connect Edward Vickers with the Stillwell case? I get two answers."

"And they are?" Quist asked, impatient.

"The answer is, 'Yes' to both questions. Edward Vickers has a record of three arrests in the last ten years, all three for assault and battery. Mr. Vickers appears to enjoy beating up people in public places. In one instance he nearly killed a man, crippled him for life, but somehow his lawyer managed to settle the case out of court for a suspiciously large sum of money—much more money than Vickers could have earned for himself in his whole lifetime. It didn't come from an insurance company, which suggests Vickers has a very rich friend somewhere. Each time he's been arrested, he's had the best of lawyers, one Max Gottfried. How do you like that for apples?"

"It ties in!" Quist said.

"I said yes was the answer to both questions," Kreevich said. "Is there anything to connect Vickers with the Stillwell case—in addition to something you smelled, friend? The monster says there is. Since I saw you, I checked out Mark Stillwell's private phone at the Westchester house. Several out-of-area calls were made the day of the murder. One of them was to Vickers' number on West Eleventh Street." Kreevich brought his fist down hard on his desk. "I want Vickers badly. I want to know where he was at the moment Jadwin was shot in Grand Central Station. I want to know what he's done with your girl."

"As sure as God he's headed for the hospital," Quist said.

"Equally as sure, he hasn't arrived there yet," Kreevich said. "You don't like police methods, do you, friend? Well, that earring you've brought me is going to get me a search warrant for Vickers' apartment. A police frame-up, right?"

"I buy it."

"Sure you do, as long as it helps you," Kreevich said. "If it didn't, you'd scream bloody murder about our underhanded methods. How far will your Miss Parmalee go for you?"

"Connie? What's she got to do with it?"

"She went to Frankel as a patient yesterday afternoon," Kreevich said. "Her doctor sent her there, suffering from acute depression, right?"

"It was a setup, you know that."

Kreevich looked at the ceiling. "This desperate girl went to the good doctor Frankel for help, and he laid his hands on her in lust. That could cost him his career."

"Who says he did any such thing?"

"Miss Parmalee will, I hope to God," Kreevich said. He lowered his eyes to Quist. "Rather than face a public charge of attempted rape on the analyst's couch, Dr. Frankel might just tell us where Mrs. Lewis has been locked away."

Quist smiled a tight smile. "You are a miserable, conniving, crooked cop," he said. "And I love you."

"Can you reach Miss Parmalee?" Kreevich asked. "The good doctor may be a little less alert at four in the morning than he will be later on."

The phone rang on Kreevich's desk and he answered it. As he listened, his face turned into an expressionless mask. "Be right there," he said finally. He put down the phone, but he didn't move.

"You were right about Vickers," he said. "He turned up at the hospital."

"They got him?" Quist asked eagerly. Vickers would know where Lydia was.

"They got him," Kreevich said, "right between the eyes. He clobbered some doctor in the hospital locker room, took his green operating suit and a face mask, made his way to the intensive care unit. I told you my man Winston was good. He spotted Vickers, stopped him, yanked the mask off his face. Vickers attacked. Winston shot him. Sonofabitch! Vickers isn't going to be able to tell us anything, ever—until the Judgment Day!"

Quist felt an almost unbearable knot in his stomach. Vickers had known where Lydia was and Vickers was dead, a hole the size of a half dollar in his forehead. Kreevich and his men were efficient—and helpless. They had saved Dan Garvey from a murderous assault, and at the same time they had lost the key to Lydia's jail.

There was more on Vickers. A homicide detective named Pucci, whose specialty was organized crime, had more on Vickers than had gone into the computer.

"I've been five years trying to wrap him up," Pucci told Kreevich and Quist. They were in the hospital morgue, looking at the huge dead body waiting for the autopsy surgeon. "He was a very cool operator, working in a field the general public doesn't know much about. I guess you'd call it industrial espionage. Vickers was the general of a small army of specialists in wire tapping, bugging, and physical violence, even an assassination or two. I thought I had him once for the murder of a union boss in the steel business. I couldn't make it stick. When a big corporation, or a conglomerate, as they call 'em, can't settle a business fight legally, they turn to professional in-fighters."

"Muscle," Quist muttered.

"Right. Muscle," Pucci said. "You ever heard of a lawyer named Max Gottfried?"

"God, have we heard of him!" Quist said.

"He always turned up when we thought we had Vickers, and he may be the best defender in the business."

"Did Vickers work for just one employer?" Kreevich asked. "Like David Lewis, for example?"

Pucci shrugged. "I never got past Gottfried," he said. "My guess is Vickers worked for anyone who could get up his fee; for me today, for you against me tomorrow." The detective's eyes narrowed. "Max Gottfried works for David Lewis, doesn't he? If Lewis needed muscle, I guess Gottfried would have recommended Vickers."

"I haven't a shred of evidence, Pucci," Kreevich said, "but I think Vickers, or one of his boys, killed Lieutenant Jadwin. I think he was guilty of kidnaping a Miss Lydia Morton. You take this end of it." He looked at Quist. "We don't need your earring now. That hunk of meat there justifies our searching his apartment."

"Will do," Pucci said.

"Not a word of this is to leak to the press or any other outside source," Kreevich said. "I'm going out to Westchester to talk to some possible employers of Vickers. I don't want Gottfried on the job till I'm ready for him. I don't want David Lewis or anyone connected with him to know what's happened. I don't want any word to leak out on Dan Garvey's condition. Understood?"

"Understood," Pucci said. "Vickers did for Garvey?"

"No question, but no proof. You can have that one,

too." Kreevich looked at Quist. "You want to ride out to the country with me? Mark Stillwell has a telephone call to explain."

"Dr. Frankel?" Quist asked.

"He'll have to wait, but I'll have him watched in case he goes to see a patient out of town—or she's brought to him."

Quist rode beside Kreevich in an unmarked police car, up the deserted East River Drive and across the Triborough Bridge. The sense of defeat was heavy on him, bathed in a blood-red rage and a need to exact a revenge for Lydia and for Dan. It had all started with pretty dresses and ended in an incredible chain of violence. He remembered Lydia and Caroline at lunch with him at Willard's Back Yard, with every eye turned toward those two lovely women, alive, gay. Both erased from the scene to save a killer's neck. An arrest, a trial, a verdict of guilty was not going to be enough to satisfy him. He wanted to inflict the pain himself.

"You're carrying a gun," Kreevich said, his eyes on the cone of light ahead of him.

"Yes," Quist said in a flat, dull voice.

"You better let me have it."

"I have a license to carry it," Quist said.

"You don't have a license to kill anyone," Kreevich said.

Quist looked at him. "You think that's what I'm thinking?"

"I know," Kreevich said. "There isn't an open season, even on murderers."

"Maybe if I think about it enough, it'll stop me from doing it. But so help me God, if Lydia and Dan—"

"Try to behave like an adult," Kreevich said. "The net is closing around them. All of them. Lewis to Gottfried to

Vickers; someone on Mark's phone to Vickers; Garvey to Vickers; Miriam Talbot frightened out of a date with Hilliard when she saw the news about Garvey, who knew about Vickers; the net is closing. Still outside it is Marcia Lewis, but we'll find her in the next few hours."

"Will she still be alive to talk?" Quist asked.

"They can't go on killing at random," Kreevich said. "They still hope to escape payment for what's already done. Question, if you can bring yourself to think sensibly. What put Garvey on Vickers' trail? It's a coincidence that they knew each other; it made Garvey handle the situation differently than if it had been someone he didn't know. But what pointed at Vickers? He came across something, looking around for a lead to what—muscle?—that took him to Vickers. Any idea at all?"

Quist tried to bring himself back to reason. "Maybe he knew that 'muscle' was his old friend's business. Maybe he thought Vickers could give him a lead to someone who might be working for Lewis, or the Stillwell crew, or both. He probably didn't dream that someone was Vickers himself."

"Interesting idea, but something gags me a little." Kreevich was hitting seventy on the Parkway. He didn't have to worry about speed cops. "If you're right, Vickers had Lydia in his apartment. He wouldn't have let anyone in, not even an old friend. He wouldn't have answered the doorbell. But something happened that made it necessary for him to wipe out Garvey. What could it have been except that Garvey knew that Lydia was there?"

"Maybe he did go down to the delicatessen, as he told me, leaving Lydia tied up there, alone. Garvey found her, but before he could free her, Vickers came back."

"How did Garvey get in? Up the fire escape and through a back window? Why would he do that unless he had something on Vickers?"

"He left a message for me," Quist said. "He had a lead, but it might not be anything."

"If he thought Lydia was there, would he have tried to make it alone? Without telling you, or me? He knew Vickers was no pushover. Would he have risked Lydia's safety by trying to be a hero?"

"It wouldn't be like him."

"So we're missing something," Kreevich said.

"We're missing Lydia," Quist said.

They drove on through the moonlit night, each man concerned with his own thoughts. Quist was asking himself what he would do—could do—if Lydia was gone forever? Behave like an adult, Kreevich had said. That's how he had been behaving until twenty-four hours ago when he'd dropped Lydia off at her apartment, expecting to see her again in a few hours. He had made a success of his business, he had made money, he had a good life style from his point of view, he had a lovely girl to share it with. Someday he would get tired of the work aspects of it and he and Lydia would travel, or buy an island somewhere. They would have earned the right to live as they chose, and love as they chose, and they would have hurt no one on the journey. Now the whole dream was fouled and destroyed by someone sick, someone evil, someone who cared only to save himself.

Quist's fingers caressed the butt of the gun that he'd slipped into his jacket pocket. He'd gotten a license for that gun because there were valuable paintings in his apartment —paintings that no insurance payment could replace if they were stolen. The law had seen fit to let him have a gun to protect his property.

He glanced at Kreevich, who was slowing down to turn off the Parkway. It was only a few miles now to the Stillwell place. There's an open season on burglars, Quist thought, but I mustn't raise a hand against the person or persons who have stolen my most valuable possession. I mustn't raise a hand against a murderer. Well, screw you, friend!

"You say something?" Kreevich asked.

"You weren't meant to hear anything," Quist said.

They drove again in silence for a while and then Quist saw the Stillwell house, high on its hillside, outlined against the sky by the moonlight.

"They better have answers," he said.

"Without answers," Kreevich said, "they will be eating to-day's breakfasts off tin plates."

The big, ivy-covered house was dark. There didn't seem to be a light anywhere. They slept, or they plotted in the dark, Quist thought.

They parked by the front door and went together up the stone steps. Kreevich rang the bell. They waited for a while and then Kreevich put his finger on the bell and held it there. At last a succession of lights popped on inside the house, each one a little closer to the front door. Finally a light went on over their heads on the outside. The door opened and Shallert, the houseman, confronted them, wearing a cotton bathrobe over pale yellow pajamas.

"Good evening—or should I say good morning—gentlemen."

"I must see Mr. Stillwell," Kreevich said. "Mr. Mark Stillwell."

Something flickered across Shallert's eyes. "I don't think he's here, Lieutenant."

"You don't think?"

"He went off somewhere in his Corvette early in the evening," Shallert said. "I haven't heard him come back. It's possible he may have. I dozed off once or twice. If you'll come in, I'll make certain, gentlemen."

"You're not sleeping well, Shallert?" Quist asked.

Shallert's face showed nothing. "It's been a restless household since the tragedy, Mr. Quist."

A woman's voice called out from the top of the wide staircase. "What is it, Shallert?" It was Beatrice Lorimer.

"It's Mr. Quist and Lieutenant Kreevich, ma'am, asking for Mr. Mark," Shallert said.

"Well, fetch him," Beatrice said.

"I don't think he's come back, ma'am."

"We want to see you all, Beatrice," Quist called out. "You, Mark, Jerry, and Patrick Grant."

"Give me a minute to change into something decent," Beatrice said. "Is there something wrong, Julian? Something new?"

"Something new," Quist said. "Will it save time if I go down to the studio for Jerry, Shallert?"

"Mr. Jerry is not here," Shallert said. "He went to New York yesterday morning. He's not expected back until the funeral, which is tomorrow. If you'll excuse me, sir, I'll see if Mr. Mark has come back—and call Mr. Grant."

They waited in the hall. In spite of its warm colors, the sunlit Wyeth painting on the far wall, it had a cold feel to it, Quist thought. Shallert took a fairly long time to report, but when he did, it was explained by the fact he'd dressed.

"As I thought, gentlemen, Mr. Mark hasn't returned," he

168

said. "I waked Mr. Grant and he'll be down in a moment."

"Did Mark say he didn't expect to come back tonight?" Quist asked.

That curious something flickered across Shallert's eyes again. "He didn't say anything to me, sir. Mrs. Lorimer will know."

And then Beatrice appeared at the head of the stairs, wearing a deep wine-colored housecoat. Not a hair was out of place, Quist saw. Not many women who needed preparation could be so prepared on such short notice. She reached Quist and put a hand on his arm.

"Not some new tragedy, Julian?" she said. "We can't take much more out here."

"Do you know where Mark Stillwell is, Mrs. Lorimer?" Kreevich asked.

"He went out for a drive earlier this evening," Beatrice said. "You must realize he's been pretty distracted. He said he just wanted to drive around—try to shake off some of the pain."

"You're not worried about him?"

"No. Should I be?"

"It's four-thirty in the morning, Mrs. Lorimer."

"He's not a child, Lieutenant. He doesn't have to check in and out with me."

Patrick Grant came down the stairs, wearing a sport shirt and slacks, with polished moccasin loafers on his feet. "Hello, Quist—Lieutenant," he said. "I take it this isn't a social call at this hour of the morning."

"Not social," Kreevich said.

"Well, at least we can sit down somewhere," Beatrice said. "Do come into the living room."

She led the way and sat down in a corner of the couch.

She gave Quist an inviting look, but he stood behind a high-backed armchair, looking down at her. The time for games is over, doll.

"Shallert, would you make some coffee, please?" Beatrice said.

The houseman slipped away. Grant had lit a cigarette and he perched himself on a corner of a long stretcher table. "Why are you here officially, Lieutenant?" he asked. He looked watchful, wary.

Kreevich had remained standing, too. "On the morning that Mrs. Stillwell was murdered, several out-of-area calls were made from this house," he said. "On the listed phone three calls were made to David Lewis's lawyer, Max Gottfried, and one to a Dr. Frankel. Mr. Gottfried has explained the calls he got. Dr. Frankel claims the privilege of the doctor-patient relationship in refusing to tell us who called him."

"I'd suppose it was David," Grant said, almost too quickly. "Marcia was hysterical. No one else needed a doctor here. David eventually got a local man, a Dr. Tabor."

"I'm aware of all that," Kreevich said. "By the way, do you or Mrs. Lorimer know where Mrs. Lewis was taken? You told Quist a sanitarium on Long Island, Mrs. Lorimer."

"That's what David said. He didn't mention the name of the place or its exact location," Beatrice said.

"Mr. Lewis should be able to tell you that without any problem," Grant said.

"Mr. Lewis has made himself inaccessible since he left here," Kreevich said. "But that wasn't the question I came here to ask." His cold eyes focused on Grant, sitting on the edge of the table, swinging a leg back and forth, squinting

170

against the smoke from his cigarette. "There were calls made from Mark Stillwell's unlisted phone."

"There were things to be done that awful morning," Grant said. "Business appointments to be canceled, one or two friends to notify. Of course there were calls."

"I'm only really interested in one of them," Kreevich said. "I'd like to know who called Edward Vickers, and why."

Grant's leg stopped swinging. His eyes narrowed.

"Who is Edward Vickers, Pat?" Beatrice asked.

"Oh, I know who Vickers is, Mrs. Lorimer," Kreevich said. "He's a professional killer, a trigger man, a seller of muscle. That's who he is, Mrs. Lorimer. My question is, who called him and why?"

Watching, Quist saw that Beatrice didn't look at Patrick Grant. It would have been natural, if she didn't know, for her to look to him for an answer.

Grant misplayed his hand. He could have denied any knowledge of Vickers, but he didn't. "That's a pretty extraordinary thing for you to say about a man—killer, trigger man, seller of muscle."

"Who called him?" Kreevich said quietly.

Grant flipped his cigarette toward the fireplace. It didn't make it. He went over, picked it up, and threw it into the bed of dead gray ashes. He was obviously playing for time.

"We believe Vickers may have murdered Lieutenant Jadwin," Kreevich said. "We wonder if he got his instructions from this house."

Grant turned. "Have you arrested Vickers?"

"No."

"You have evidence against him?"

"We know he got a call from here," Kreevich said. "We

know his lawyer is Max Gottfried, who got calls from here. It would help us a lot to know who called him from here and why, Mr. Grant."

Grant lit a fresh cigarette. "I called him," he said.

"Pat!" Beatrice cried out. Her surprise sounded false.

"Why?" Kreevich asked in his flat, level voice.

Grant had made up his mind how to answer. It came easy now. "Mark and I had an appointment to see Vickers that morning in New York. Obviously we couldn't keep the appointment. I called Vickers to cancel it."

"Polite of you," Kreevich said dryly. "What business did you and Mark Stillwell have with Vickers?"

"I don't believe I'm required to answer that, Lieutenant."

"Then if I assume you really called Vickers to tell him to get rid of Lieutenant Jadwin, you won't be offended?"

"That's absurd, Lieutenant," Beatrice said. Pallor was showing through her careful make-up.

Grant was still hanging in there. "There are some strange twists and turns in the management of big business, Lieutenant," he said. "I knew of Vickers as a sort of detective; you might call him an industrial spy. We needed his services to get information about a certain corporation before we completed a merger with them."

"It's been a long day and night," Kreevich said. "I'm really not interested in all this embroidery work, Mr. Grant."

Grant tried a small smile. "I can't help it if you don't believe the truth, Lieutenant."

Quist spoke. "You had a date for a night on the town with Gloria Chard, one of my researchers," he said. "You didn't keep it. Why?"

Grant shrugged. "Business complications piled up on me."

"And you came out here to settle them? Were you so upset when you heard what Vickers had done to Dan Garvey, my partner, that you had to get out here to warn Beatrice and Mark that there might be trouble?"

"I don't know what you're talking about," Grant said.

"Where is Lydia?" Quist demanded, and his voice shook.

Grant's smile disappeared. "What does that mean? How would I know where Lydia is? Don't you know?"

"You know," Quist said, "because Vickers was your man and Vickers had her."

"You're off your rocker," Grant said.

Kreevich sighed. "As I said, it's been a long day and night. I'm putting an end to this part of it by placing you both under arrest, charged with conspiracy to commit a homicide."

"I have a right to call my lawyer," Grant said.

"Sure, only don't call Max Gottfried," Kreevich said. "I'm having him picked up, too. There's a telephone in the entrance hall, I believe." He turned and walked out of the room.

Beatrice was on her feet, reaching out to Quist. "Julian, this is madness! Surely you don't think—"

"I think, as the Lieutenant put it to me so aptly, Beatrice, you're all going to spend a long time eating your meals off tin plates. Unless—"

"Unless what, Julian?" She touched his hands and her fingers were ice-cold.

"You're covering up for someone," Quist said. "Is it David Lewis? Is it Mark—your storefront window dressing? What did Marcia Lewis see, and where is she so we can ask her?"

"I told you, Julian, someplace on Long Island."

"I don't believe you. I don't believe anything either of you has said so far. I'll concede you one thing. This whole horror has snowballed out of all proportion to what you thought you were doing when it started. My partner, Garvey, may not live because of Vickers. Lydia may be dead because of Vickers. Vickers is your man. I think you know who killed Caroline, know who put gasoline in Johnny Tiptoe's car, know that it was Vickers who killed Lieutenant Jadwin, know where Marcia Lewis is. I don't know what the police or the courts will do to you, but I know that if Dan dies and Lydia doesn't get back to me safe, you will have to kill me, too, to save yourselves from me."

"Julian!"

"Where is Marcia Lewis?"

"I told you, someplace on Long Island."

"I don't believe you. Where is Mark? Rolling around in the hay somewhere with Miriam Talbot? He doesn't have to come home, does he, now that Caroline is dead?"

Kreevich came back from the front hall. "Lieutenant Sims is on his way," he said. "You can pack a bag to take to jail with you, Mrs. Lorimer."

"You and Quist have invented a fairy story," Grant said. "There isn't one shred of proof against us—any of us!"

"Then your lawyer will spring you," Kreevich said. "But there is a second charge I'll bring against you. You are helping to hide Marcia Lewis, the witness to a murder."

Beatrice turned to Grant. "Pat, is there any reason why—?"

"Shut up, Beatrice!"

"Mark! What about Mark?" Beatrice said.

"Lieutenant Sims will pick him up on the way here,"

Kreevich said. "He is at Bayne's cottage with Miss Talbot, isn't he?"

Beatrice moved unsteadily toward the door of the room. There she turned. "Julian, tell Lydia I'm sorry."

"Will you keep your mouth shut, Beatrice!" Grant shouted.

"How can I tell Lydia anything if I can't find her?" Quist asked, his voice rising.

Beatrice just shook her head and headed for the stairway.

"You can make your lawyer call, and that's all, Mr. Grant," Kreevich said.

Half an hour later Sims arrived with a shattered-looking Mark. Kreevich's guess had evidently been correct. To Quist's surprise, Kreevich had no intention of staying in Westchester to work on his prisoners. Instead he insisted that Quist join him on a trip back to New York.

"You're giving them time to build even bigger lies!" Quist protested. "Beatrice knows something about Lydia. Give me some time with her!"

"When this case is closed, your Lydia will be safe, and not before," Kreevich said. "So let's close it."

"How?"

Kreevich started the car and bluestone scattered under his abrupt start. "I couldn't prevent Grant the right to call his lawyer," he said. "It was a man named Maidstone, a partner in Gottfried's firm—as if that was a surprise. Grant told Maidstone they were being arrested on a conspiracy charge, nothing else."

"So?"

"All he had to do, Julian, was make a call. It didn't matter what he said. A call was a message. We are onto them, and some plan of action had to be set in motion."

"What plan? What are you talking about?"

"Contingency plan. We suspect, we have guessed most of the truth, but we haven't one shred of evidence. In a few hours Maidstone will have them out on bail with an airtight story ready for us. Without Marcia Lewis they have us beaten for the time being. Vickers will become the fall guy if it goes that far. Grant would be laughing at us if he knew Vickers was dead.

"But we don't know how to find Marcia Lewis!"

"We know one thing for sure," Kreevich said. "She's nowhere on Long Island, because that's where they say she is." He reached down and took up the telephone on his car dash. He dialed, and a monotonous voice came over the speaker. "Lieutenant Kreevich here. I want a search and seizure warrant for the residence of Dr. Milton Frankel on Park Avenue. I'll be there in forty minutes."

"It may be tough to get one so fast," the voice said.

"I want it there," Kreevich said. "And I want the doctor's building covered as of now. I want to know who goes in, who goes out. If they bring out a woman about forty years old—" He glanced at Quist.

"Blonde, bone-thin," Quist said.

"Blonde, very thin," Kreevich said into the phone. "If they bring her out, I want her followed. If you lose her, you'll lose your head. Get to it."

He drove now, very fast when he hit the Parkway. It was still not light, but in the east there was a faint red glow beginning to show.

"Money buys almost anything," Kreevich said. "A lawyer, a doctor, a killer. That's what you can buy with

176

enough money. So far Marcia Lewis has been safe because Lewis cares for her, in his way. But if it comes to a showdown, she will, I suspect, die of an overdose of some sedative, some sleeping medicine. But not in the good doctor's house. That would make things too sticky for him."

"They'll kill her?"

"Who won't they kill to save their hides?" Kreevich said. "She knows who started all this by carving up Caroline Stillwell. Let's hope we can get to her first." He pounded the wheel with a clenched fist. "If I could answer two questions, I might be able to do without her. What took Caroline Stillwell down to the pool that night? And what put Garvey on Vickers' trail?"

They were just approaching the Triborough Bridge when Kreevich's car phone buzzed.

"Warrant's ready for you, Lieutenant, and the Park Avenue house is staked out. No action so far."

"I'll be there in ten or twelve minutes," Kreevich said, and stepped down harder on the gas.

They raced through the deserted city streets. Street lights were still on, but dawn was creeping over the towers of the town. They turned south on Park Avenue and a moment or two later, skipping through stoplights, they approached Frankel's building. There was a large black limousine parked in front of the house. At the end of the block was another car which Quist guessed was an unmarked police vehicle. Kreevich drew up alongside it.

"Glad you got here, Lieutenant," a plainclothes man said. "Looks like something's cooking." Quist recognized Pucci, the officer he'd met at the hospital. "Three men just drove up in that limousine and went into the house. One of them was David Lewis. I know him from pictures."

"Let's go," Kreevich said. "You got the warrant?"

Pucci slapped his pocket. Kreevich parked and he and Pucci and Quist started across the street. Before they reached the limousine, the front door of the house opened and a group of people emerged. David Lewis was walking on one side of his wife, a strange man on the other. They seemed to be supporting a dead weight. A third man hurried to open the rear door of the limousine.

"That will be just about far enough, Mr. Lewis," Kreevich said.

The little cavalcade seemed to freeze. Glancing up at the house, Quist caught a glimpse of Dr. Frankel inside the door, which was abruptly slammed shut. Kreevich and Pucci moved forward, and then it began to happen. The two men with the Lewises drew guns. Pucci dove for the protection of the limousine, fumbling for his own gun. Kreevich did the unbelievable. He charged straight at Lewis and his wife. Quist saw him stagger as he was hit, but he kept on, threw himself on top of Marcia Lewis, knocking her down onto the steps of the house and covering her body with his. One of the gunmen was down and the other was concentrating on Pucci.

Quist reached the steps and pressed the cold barrel of his gun against the side of David Lewis's neck.

"Call them off, Lewis," he said, "or I'll blow off your head!"

It was too late to call anyone off. Pucci had nailed the second man, who was writhing on the pavement. Quist knelt beside Kreevich and a screaming Marcia Lewis. Kreevich turned his head and his face was twisted with pain.

"I thought they'd shoot her right in front of us!" he said.

178

"How badly are you hit?"

"Shoulder. Not too bad—but awfully damn close!"

He struggled up to his feet, clutching at his right arm. Quist helped the hysterical Marcia up. Lewis, like a statue, hadn't moved. The door to the house opened and Dr. Frankel stood there.

"Oh, my God!" he said. "Oh, my God!"

Pucci was at a police box, calling for help and an ambulance.

"I think we'd better take your patient back into the house, Doctor," Kreevich said.

"I've got to tell someone! I've got to tell!" Marcia screamed. "I killed her! Do you hear me, I killed her!"

David Lewis looked like a man who was witnessing the end of the world. He sat in a big armchair in Dr. Frankel's consulting room. The doctor, after a quick, reassuring look at Kreevich's wound, had taken Marcia Lewis somewhere else.

"She can't talk," Frankel said. "She's in no condition to make any sense. Maybe later, if I can quiet her—"

"It doesn't matter," Lewis said in a dull voice. "I can tell you all that she can tell you. There's no point in trying to hide anything any more."

His mountain had crumbled.

Quist was fighting to keep from asking the critical question for him. Lewis was going to have to tell it his own way, or his mood might change.

"It may be hard for you to believe, in view of what I have to tell you, but I love Marcia. God help her. We started together when she was so young—and so lovely. But she was never really part of my world except in our personal intimacy. She never cared for what was really my life—money and power. Marcia—poor child—began to drift away from reality entirely. Dr. Frankel tried to help her, and sometimes it was better, more often it was worse. The doctor warned me over and over again that she was psychotic, should be put away, but I couldn't do that to her. I kept her with me, guarded her as best I could from herself."

Come on, Quist thought. For God sake, get to it and to Lydia.

"There was never anything I couldn't get in this world because I had the power to demand it or the money to buy it," Lewis said. "Women! There was no sex life left with Marcia, and I was hungry for it." He stopped as though he had run out of the strength to continue.

"Caroline Stillwell?" Kreevich asked quietly.

Lewis nodded. He opened his mouth but no words came. He tried again. "God, she was lovely," he said. "I watched her all that evening of the party and I knew I—I had to have her. I went to her room when everyone else had retired. I said I needed her, wanted her, had to have her. She was angry because I had barged in and found her undressing, just wearing her bra and panties. She picked up a robe and covered herself, demanding that I go away at once. She didn't scream or try to denounce me, because she knew how important I was to Mark. I knew she knew that. I put it to her very matter-of-factly. If she would let me make love to her, I'd give Mark anything he wanted. I'd make him king of the world—next to me. She loved Mark. I thought she would do anything for him. But she ordered me out."

He hadn't known or understood Caroline, Quist thought.

Hadn't known her at all.

Lewis moistened lips that were dry and pale. "I—I had to have her. I knew Mark well enough to know I could silence him—afterwards. Mark is nothing. Beatrice and Pat Grant are the power there. They'd all wash it out for what I could give them. I—I tried to force myself on Caroline. And at that moment Marcia burst into the room." Lewis covered his face with his hands. "Oh, God!"

They waited for him to go on.

"Marcia was wild with rage. She called Caroline filthy names—called her a whore, a teaser. She tried to get at Caroline, but I held her off. Then she broke away from me, saying that she was going to kill herself, and ran out of the room." Little beads of sweat had broken out on Lewis's forehead. "That was that. I'd heard Marcia threaten suicide a hundred times, so I wasn't too concerned. The moment with Caroline, however, was passed. I went back to my own room. The next thing that happened I only know from what poor Marcia has told me."

"She was going to kill herself?" Kreevich asked.

"You'd have to live with that kind of distorted mind, Lieutenant, to understand it," Lewis said. "You have to understand that it wasn't sexual jealousy that had her in such a state. Long ago it was understood between us that I couldn't be physically faithful to her. What drove Marcia into such a wild state was fear that I would desert her, that she'd be left alone. She was almost more afraid to live than she was to die. If I deserted her, she believed she would be put away, restrained, treated as a mad person." Lewis wiped at his face. "I knew her so well I didn't believe she meant to kill herself. I know now she went down into the kitchen and found a butcher knife. I think she thought I would follow her, stop her. That would reassure her. She ran out into the garden with it."

"And Caroline saw her?" Quist asked.

"Yes. She ran down to the pool to stop Marcia from harming herself."

There was one unanswered question answered, Quist thought.

"Mad people can generate extraordinary strength," Lewis said. "Marcia turned on Caroline, hating her with a passion, and she—she—"

"Killed her," Kreevich said, putting a period to it.

"Marcia came back to the house, carrying the bloody knife, and ran head on into Patrick Grant. She—she wasn't hiding anything. She told him what she'd done. At that moment she wanted to tell the whole world! Grant silenced her somehow, got her upstairs to me. He took away the knife to clean it. Then he went down and looked at Caroline. It was too late to do anything for her. That was the key to it—too late to do anything for Caroline.

"I wasn't myself at that moment, not really in control. Grant and Mark took me aside to talk to me. I'd managed to get Marcia to bed under sedation. It was awful, they said, but there was nothing to be gained by exposing Marcia. The police would find another explanation for it. The scandal would be damaging to me in the business world. They would play along—for a price."

"Mark to be made head of the Sports Complex?" Quist asked.

"In name, at least. It would mean that Grant and Beatrice would actually control it. I—God help me—agreed. That was why I made the announcement at what was obviously a bad time, Quist. They had to be assured I'd keep my word. I actually signed a contract with them before you and Miss Morton found Caroline's body.

"It seemed, almost at once, that we'd had a marvelous break. The Tiptoe boy was arrested. Just to be sure it would hold up, Grant put gas in the boy's car, not knowing that Hilliard had already checked it out empty. You turned Jadwin's attention to us, Mr. Quist, and we were all seized by a kind of desperate panic. I got Marcia away here to Dr. Frankel. It was while I was gone that Grant lost his head. Jadwin had to be stopped. You had to be stopped. I wasn't there to be consulted. He hired the man Vickers to do away with Jadwin and kidnap Miss Morton to get you out of the act.

"It was a piece of incredible stupidity, but we were all stuck with it. I told Grant no more killings or I would turn myself and Marcia in. He promised me."

"Where is Lydia!" Quist shouted. His voice reverberated around the room.

"I don't know," Lewis said. "The whole thing got out of my control. I heard last night from Gottfried that Vickers had killed your friend Garvey." A great sob shook him. I found that I was a coward, Quist. I couldn't turn myself in. I decided I would take Marcia away, somewhere to the end of the earth. I hired two of Vickers' men to help me get her away. In a few days Frankel could have admitted that she'd been here. He'd committed no crime. He took care of his patient as best he could."

"And was well paid for it," Quist said bitterly.

The telephone rang on the doctor's desk and Kreevich answered it. A strange look came over his face. He held out the receiver to Quist. "For you," he said. "They found you through me."

News of Garvey, Quist thought. Bad news?

"Yes?" he said.

"Darling!"

The room began to spin around him.

"Lydia! Oh, my God, where are you?"

"At your apartment, love."

"Are you all right?"

"I'm fine. Just fine, darling. Could you hurry, do you think?"

She was there!

She melted into his arms and he held her, almost painfully tight. All he could say for a long time was her name, over and over.

"It's all right, darling. It's all right," she said, her hands stroking his face, his hair.

At last he held her away at arm's length. "You're not hurt?"

"No. You may not believe it, Julian, but I was free to walk away any time I chose."

"Then why in God's name—?"

"You are to sit down in that chair," she said, "and I will bring you a drink, and I will give you just that much time to talk. And then—"

"Then I will take charge," Quist said. "Oh, God, it's good to see you all in one piece."

Lydia worked at the bar with ice and whiskey. "After you dropped me at my apartment, I'd just had time to shower and change—I was going to meet you at the office, you remember—when the doorbell rang and I found myself confronted by this giant man, Ed Vickers. I know from Connie that you know about him."

"Do you know that he's dead? He tried to get at Dan in the hospital and the cops shot him. But tell me what happened to you."

"Vickers was very persuasive. Not physical, but persuasive. If I cared for you, I would do exactly what he told me. I was to disappear. You would read that as a message warning you to back away from the Stillwell case. If you were a good boy and took the hint, I would sooner or later be released. If I didn't play along with him you'd be gunned down the next time you put your nose outside this house." Lydia brought his drink across to him. "I didn't think he was bluffing, Julian."

"He wasn't," Quist said. He sipped the drink. It tasted marvelous, as though her having made it, a special nectar had been added to it.

"He took me to his apartment on Eleventh Street," Lydia said. "Nothing unpleasant, no passes. It was strictly business with him. He went out from time to time. 'There's the phone,' he said. 'You can call for help, or you can walk out the front door. But if you do, you won't see Quist again alive.'" Lydia bent down and kissed Quist's cheek. "I very much wanted to see you alive again, darling. And so, believe it or not, I just sat and waited, a prisoner of my own choice. The phone was hell; it made you seem so close. But I thought somehow he'd know if I called you."

"Dan. Where does Dan come in?" Quist asked.

"Dan came in through the bedroom window," Lydia said. "Vickers had gone out to the delicatessen to buy some sandwiches. He made sure I didn't starve, but he wasn't much of a cook. And there was Dan, coming through the window. He tried to drag me away, and I had almost to fight him off to make him listen. If I went with him, you might be killed. I kept asking him how he happened to find me, at the same time urging him to go before Vickers got back."

"How did he find you?"

"He wasn't looking for me. He was as surprised to find me as I was to see him. Dan had been doing a rundown on Patrick Grant. He discovered that a friend of his—old college chum—sold Grant his personal insurance. While they were talking, the friend told Dan that another old college chum, Ed Vickers, worked for Grant. He'd run into Grant and Vickers in some Greenwich Village bar. They'd rapped for a while about the good old days at State."

"And Dan knew the kind of work Vickers did?"

"Right. He was looking for muscle that Lewis or Mark might use, and his old friend Vickers fitted the bill perfectly. He'd waited around for Vickers to go out—to the delicatessen—and he'd come up the fire escape, hoping that he'd find something, some paper or letters, that would tie Vickers to the Stillwells or Lewis. He never dreamed he was going to find me. And then we heard Vickers' key in the door. Dan went back through the window but not quite quick enough. Vickers almost caught him right there. He chased Dan down the fire escape and, unhappily caught him in the alley. When he came back, he was white with anger. 'Your boy friend isn't getting the message,' he said. He made a phone call of which I couldn't make any sense. Then he told me he had to take me somewhere else. Dan might have left word where he was coming. He took me to an apartment uptown. When I was alone, it didn't take me long to find out whose apartment it was. Miriam Talbot's!"

"You saw her?"

"No, but there were letters, a picture of Mark Stillwell."

"We've got them all," Quist said. He gave her a quick run-down on what had happened.

He put down his empty glass. "I'm going to call the hospital for a report on Dan," he said, "and then, my lovely, I take charge."

"I called the hospital just before you got here," Lydia said. "Dan's improved. You can't talk to him yet, though. So—"

"So what are we waiting for?" Quist said. He put his arm around her and led her toward the circular stairway.